MW00476669

ROMANCE ON THE ORIENT EXPRESS

A Novel

ANTHONY MCDONALD

Anchor Mill Publishing

Anchor Mill Publishing

4/04 Anchor Mill

Paisley PA1 1JR

SCOTLAND

anchormillpublishing@gmail.com

Cover design by Barry Creasy

For Steve Gee as always

Author's Note

In February 1929 an Orient Express train ploughed into a snowdrift in Eastern Thrace, European Turkey, just sixty miles short of its destination of Constantinople. Passengers and crew endured extremes of cold, hunger and other hardships before rescue arrived after some six days. The event captured the front pages of newspapers around the world, and also the imagination of Agatha Christie. Nearly three years later she herself was stranded for twenty-four hours in Croatia on a northbound Express, after heavy rain and floods had washed away a section of track. A synthesis of the two events became the background setting for her classic, Murder on the Orient Express.

I too have borrowed elements from both those true stories, as well as some incidental detail – with affection and respect – from Mrs Christie's book. Romance on the Orient Express is, however, a work of fiction, just as Mrs Christie's classic is.

In researching the background to my story I found the following books enormously informative, as well as inspiring and entertaining. Graham Greene: Stamboul Train. First published 1932. Agatha Christie: Murder on the Orient Express. First published 1934. E. H. Cookridge: Orient Express. First published 1978. Ali: Two Gay Muslim Couples. Published 2014

Anthony McDonald

ONE

Braslav...

Belgrade was the hub. The centre of my world. All right, it was where I lived. It was where I worked.

At least, it was where I started my working day. And usually, though not always, where I ended it. I drove trains. To Subatica, in the direction of Hungary. To Zagreb. Across the border with Bulgaria sometimes, to Sofia. Sometimes to the north-west tip of my 57-varieties country, to Trieste. Trieste was the gateway to Italy, and to everything that lay beyond that. France. England. Spain. The United States...

I drove the Orient Express.

Don't misunderstand me. Because of events that happened, and books that were written afterwards, and

1

the romance that got attached to that, some people imagine the Orient Express as a single train, made up of a single set of carriages, a single locomotive, and perhaps a heroic driver and fireman who took the thing from Istanbul to London, a journey of three whole days, working day and night without a wink of sleep.

The reality was a bit different. The Orient Express was – and has been, and from time to time still is – a network of routes criss-crossing Europe. The routes converged and diverged: carriages were added and detached. Drivers and firemen joined the trains at the international borders, then left again as the next border was reached. Locomotives were detached and replaced. No country on our continent of unending conflicts wanted to find its expensive equipment stuck on the wrong side of the border if a war broke out. Furthermore, there was a daily service. It departed from Istanbul at ten in the evening, I think, during the years I was driving my bit of the route. It arrived in Belgrade just under twenty-four hours later. At 8.45 pm to be precise. It left again exactly thirty minutes later. I do of course remember that, because that was when I took charge of it.

Because of the layout of the Belgrade Glavna station – it was a terminus – the train arrived and left by the same route. Any passengers who had gone to sleep in the early evening facing the engine would wake to find themselves facing away from it. Usually a Bulgarian 4-6-2 drew the carriages into the platform, was uncoupled, and we reversed a similar, though Yugoslavian registered, engine down onto the other end of it.

Though not immediately. A bit of shunting had to be done first. A couple of carriages bound for Bucharest, and carrying passengers who were making their way to Berlin or Prague or Paris Gare de l'Est, were removed from the train and sided before being attached to another one. Likewise, other cars that had come from Athens were added to the train. Was I standing watching all this? Rarely. I had work to do. I was in the locomotive yard a couple of miles away from Glavna. It was there, and on this particular day that I first clapped my eyes on Nedim.

Nedim...

'Something different for you tomorrow,' Jusuf said to me when I clocked on for my day's work at four o'clock in the morning, in the snow and the pitch dark. 'You're going on the Orient Express.'

'The Orient Express?' I said to him in astonishment. 'I've never done that.' I didn't literally quake in my boots. It just felt like I was doing it.

Jusuf took the pencil he always carried behind his ear and twirled it in his fingers for a second before replacing it. 'The world wasn't built by people who never did things they hadn't done before. Grow up, for heaven's sake. Orient Express, Orient Express. It's just a train. You shovel coal till you feel your lungs are going to burst. You look out of the window, watch the signals – we give you the route map of the signals along the way –

3

and you report to the driver if any of them are at red. Just like any other train. Like any day of the week. It's hardly automobile science. Oh, and you'll get a border pass, stamped by the Compagnie Internationale des Wagons-Lits to show at the border before Trieste. We'll give you that. Don't lose it.'

Today I would be spending my day like any other day. On trains that were pulled by saddle-tanks in and out of the Belgrade suburbs. Shovelling coal, as Jusuf had said, and reading the signal aspects. Signal arm pointing down meant go in those days. Arm pointing up meant stop.

'You're a big girl, Nedim,' I heard Jusuf say. 'Physique of a god and with the strength of an ox. But there's just a little girl inside of you. You need to sort that out. Get a grip.' He turned his back on me and walked off, presumably to go and bawl at someone else. I walked off in the other direction to find saddle-tank number 80566, meet its driver and get the firebox lit. I cursed Jusuf under my breath. Nobody loves the foreman. But I had to admit he had a point. I did have a problem with that side of myself. I couldn't have put it into words. But I knew what it was.

I hardly slept that night. My mind went through all the what-ifs of a day that would be spent travelling to the furthest end of Yugoslavia, across the new border into a town, Trieste, that had now become a part of Italy, and back. I had never travelled so far in all my life. Would I need to take a day's supply of food with me? Would they know what a sausage was in Trieste? Did they only eat noodles there, as I'd heard the population of Italy did? If I had to eat noodles, would I be able to manage that without gagging and throwing up?

I was back at the yard at three in the morning, in the knee-cramping, lung-punching cold, crunching over new snow in the dark blue dark. 'Looking for 4-6-2, number 72619. Loco for the Orient Express,' I said to the man at the yard gate.

He looked at me strangely. 'You're twelve hours early,' he said. 'Light up at four this afternoon. Roll out at half-past eight.' He gave me a grin that had a bit of a leer in it. 'You get on home and go back to bed. Give her a bit of it.'

There wasn't a her, of course. I didn't even give myself a bit of it.

Twelve hours later I was back. Obviously – though I was grateful for this – there was a different man on the gate. I found 72619. If you've been a passenger on a steam train you've probably stood on the platform and admired the locomotive. But you've seen only half of it: the top half. Standing on the ground and looking up at a big steam engine, though... Well, they're mountainous. 72619 had two steam-collecting domes, a short un-frilled funnel and a headlamp in the centre of the boiler door at the front. She was also equipped with the most modern gadgetry: sand-boxes, and an array of gears and valves linked to the piston- and connecting-rods that I didn't even know the names of. I thought 72619 was one of the most beautiful things I'd seen in my life.

Then a man came into view, walking round the front of the engine from the other side, clad in overalls like I was, and carrying an oil-can. Along with the oil-can he had an air of authority and confidence. We stared into each other's faces. Something happened at that moment. I didn't know what it was. I had the impression of a lightning flash. This was my first sight of Braslav, the driver I would share the footplate with today. I didn't know what had happened; that was true. But I did know that, whatever it was, it had happened to both of us.

'You're early,' he said. 'Good man.' He named himself. 'Braslav.'

I said, 'Nedim.'

He astonished me by smiling gloriously and repeating my name back to me. 'Nedim,' he said, as though he liked the sound of it.

I was dim. I couldn't imagine why he might like the sound of my name. Why he might be happy to meet me.

'I'll light up,' I said.

There was no magic involved in the lighting of the fire in a steam engine's firebox. It was like lighting a fire in a domestic grate. It was just that afterwards it grew fifty times as big. I walked off and grabbed the nearest wheelbarrow that wasn't actually being held by someone else and filled it from the bunker of split planks and sleepers that we used for kindling. Braslav helped me lift the barrow up onto the footplate, from where I tipped the contents into the firebox. I stuffed an oily rag in underneath the pile of sticks and set light to it, then ran off at breakneck speed to fill the barrow with small pieces of coal that were kept in another bunker inside the shed.

Back at 72619 Braslav and I repeated the process. I didn't need to return the wheelbarrow. As soon as I dropped it to the ground another fireman called, 'Oy, mate, give me that,' and took it literally out of my hands.

We had enough water and coal for start-up. As the small coal pieces flamed into life I began to pile on shovels-full of the big stuff. I felt the sweat begin to pour out of me. Then I felt Braslav's hand on my shoulder. 'Easy up,' he said. 'Let's get a coffee while the bugger warms up.'

We had coffee in the crew mess which was annexed to the engine repair shed. There was a small crowd of other firemen and drivers in there, some of whom I knew, some I didn't. At first I found myself wondering why I'd never bumped into Braslav before. Then the penny dropped. I knew him well enough by sight. But always from a distance. He was a driver on the Simplon Orient Express after all. I'd been in awe of him and had never tried to get up close.

Braslav...

Why had I not noticed this handsome fellow before? As I stood drinking coffee with him at the zinc counter in the mess it came to me that of course I'd seen him. He was a fireman who worked on the saddle-tanks that hauled the local traffic. In and out of the Belgrade suburbs every day. Why had I never tried to talk to him? It wasn't that I had any snobbish regard for the difference in our rank and status. It was something very different from that. The truth was that I had seen him often; I had found him so beautiful that I hadn't been able to admit that to myself; it was far too complicated; I had managed to blank the sight of him and the thought of him out. Today I would not be able to do this. We would share the footplate for the nearly twelve hours it took to get to Trieste. There we would get our heads down in a railwaymen's hostel for a dozen hours or so, and then prepare the engine again, ready for the drive back.

Getting our heads down in a *pensione*... My mind boggled rather at that. It was something I did often enough with other firemen. And, yes, temptation did occasionally present itself. But it was temptation on one side only. It had to be resisted anyway: the consequences of not resisting it would have been too terrible to contemplate. However, today there was one big difference. Never before had I shared a footplate – let alone a room in a *pensione* – with someone as beautiful as this. 'Your name again?' I asked him as we drained the syrupy black coffee from our glasses. 'Nedim,' he reminded me. Nedim. Nedim, of course.

'You're not from round here, are you,' I said as we returned, scrunching fresh snow, to our locomotive.

'Neither are you,' he said.

'No,' I admitted, and for the first time in my life I felt awkward about admitting this. 'I'm from Croatia. That makes me a Roman Catholic.'

'And I,' said Nedim, 'as you've already guessed, am a Bosnian. Muslim, of course.'

It was for me to say what had to be said next. I was the senior crewman. Also, I guessed, I was about three years older (at thirty-one) than Nedim was. I smiled into his eyes to show that I was going to speak lightly. 'It takes all sorts to make a world,' I said.

My words had a bigger effect on him than I could have imagined in advance. He grinned at me in a way that suggested a childlike delight. And, despite the fact that we were walking fast and purposefully side by side, he swung towards me and shook my hand. 'Oh man,' he said. 'You've made me so happy by saying that.' Then, as though he felt suddenly that he'd been too forward with his enthusiasm, shrank away from me and scowled and then looked sheepish.

I now was filled with a childlike kind of delight myself, but I knew I would have to be careful how I expressed it. I said, choosing my words and my tone as if handling bantam eggs, 'I think we shall make a great team.' I had no idea as I uttered the words of how big and deep a prophecy that was.

TWO

Nedim...

The snow began to fall more thickly as the dusk faded to evening gloom and the lights came on, glowing yellow-white in the railway yards. People talk of snow falling heavily. But snow never falls heavily. It is always light on its feet, like the dancers in a ballet. Like the swans in Swan Lake. It swirled about us like white moss as we trundled across the points to the turn-table; while we pulled 72619 slowly round till she faced in the opposite direction, took her to the water-tower to fill her tanks, then positioned her under the coal hopper to fill her tender up. Next came the patient crawl backwards for two miles, tender-first, towards the platform at Glavna where the uncoupled carriages of the Orient Express awaited us.

The ground was already carpeted with white. The rails, standing proud above their invisible sleepers, shone like graphite: parallel pencil sweeps on a canvas from which all else had been erased by the snow's light touch. As we wound our way slowly along the track and through the maze of multiple points I stood looking down the side of the tender towards the signals that we passed. Seven feet away Braslav had his head out on the other side, doing exactly the same thing. Behind his back he held the long arm of the regulator in a light grip. For the moment I didn't even have as much to do as that. The fire was piled high enough to make the limited amount of steam we needed for this cautious backwards trip. I had no need, for the moment, to go on heaping it up.

The platforms opened up in front of us as we rounded the last curve, spilling the yellow light of the station towards us from under the canopied roof. Hands still behind his back Braslav casually pulled on the lever of the steam-pressure brake. We came to a stop just six inches from the buffers of the line of carriages that waited for us.

The station crew were on the platform ready. They signed to us. Braslav released the brake, touched the regulator with the lightest movement of his hand, and the tender nosed its way six inches, and a bit more, into the buffers of the carriage nearest us. There was a grunt, a squeal, a shudder. We stopped. The coupling chain was attached and clinched. The steam pipe that would supply braking power as well as heat to the whole train was unfastened and screwed tightly into the connecting pipe that dangled from the coach. The train had a corridor that connected all the carriages. Some engines these days had corridor tenders that linked up to the train. Ours did not. The corridor attachment was left untouched.

Braslav got out onto the platform to check the attachment. I began to heap the fire up. Braslav climbed back in. 'Cold night ahead of us,' he said. It was the coldest winter for a generation, everyone said; we both knew that. 'You going to be warm enough?' He smiled at me in a way I found unusual. I was unexpectedly touched by that.

'Hope so,' I said. I had long-johns and a sweater under my boiler suit, two pairs of thick socks inside my boots, a waterproof jacket over the top and a shiny leather peaked cap. Braslav appeared to be identically clad as far as I could tell. I wouldn't have known if he had the long-johns, of course, and obviously I wasn't going to ask. We both had knapsacks, which were almost identical, containing – in the case of mine, bread and cold sausage, and a flask of coffee with lots of sugar in it. I guessed that Braslav's was similarly filled: again, I wasn't going to ask. I guessed that Braslav was about three years older than I was. As I saw him climbing back up from the platform to join me on the footplate I had the most wonderful yet dismaying feeling in the depths of me. I knew that he was the most beautiful creature I had ever encountered in my life. And I had no experience to look back on that could guide me or could help me handle that.

But we had a job to get on with. After a few minutes our signal flopped down and turned to green and the *chef de train*, the chief conductor, on the platform in the distance, held his flag at the ready. He whistled. Braslav pulled the chain ring downwards and our engine screeched deafeningly back. The green flag dropped. Already Braslav had wound back the cut-off and released the brake. Now he inched the regulator open on its long lever. The first fast piston strokes hammered out, their exhausts filling the smoke-box with echoing bangs, while the air filled with a mixture of white steam and black smoke over our heads. Braslav held the regulator patiently and a second or two later the wheels began to bite, the rapid banging replaced by steady powerful chuffs. 72619 was gaining traction and slowly, surely, moving ahead. I was travelling for the first time in my life on the Orient Express. I stopped shovelling and grinned my moment's exhilaration across at Braslav. To my surprise he was looking directly at me. Our two grins met, then grew together. I knew at that moment that something extraordinary had happened; I just didn't know what it was.

Braslav...

That grin he gave me. The grin of a big angel with a coal-streaked face. Something happened to me at that moment. I knew what it was. I would have to tread carefully with this.

Nedim...

We threaded our way through the skein of tracks and points, bearing gradually right, towards the north and west. At first, while we were still within the city and its outskirts there were lamps high above us at the side of the track. But as we left the built-up area behind us the lamps ceased. Our own oil-fuelled headlight shone ahead of us, but dimly, as a pocket torch lights your way in deep countryside at night. On a clear night it would show the rails like mercury capillaries running a couple of hundred yards ahead. That distance was nothing like our braking distance, but a big steam engine with a train behind it will never come across anything big enough to derail it or halt it in its tracks. Not a deer, a horse, or even a bus. The only thing that could do damage would be another steam train coming the other way. That never happens these days. Signals were invented precisely in order to deal with that.

Even on a clear night this countryside would be dark. We were running up the broad valley of the Danube: it was an un-peopled place. But tonight our headlight showed just swirls of falling snow that looked like fog. The silver threads of our plate-way shone back at us only intermittently and from time to time we could hear, through the clatter of wheels and piston-blasts, a gentler sound like the soft tearing of silk. A second later a splash of snow would slap against the side of the cab; then a little taste of it would slide in beneath the folding waist-high partition that was set between the engine and the tender to stop us falling out. This happened at every point where the snow lay deeper than the rails' height.

We talked about the snow, in a rather unengaged and aimless way, like strangers in a coffee shop who feel they should at least talk about something, however banal it is. From time to time we touched against each other by accident in our confined though open-to-the-winds working space. We half-muttered *'pardon'* each time out of polite habit. But I for my part wasn't sorry. Each time it happened I got a good feeling from it. On top of the other feelings I'd had in connection with Braslav at every juncture in the course of our short acquaintanceship this was giving me quite a lot to think about. I had never had sex with a man although half-guiltily I'd often wanted to. But neither had I ever spent twelve hours cooped up in a driver's cab with a man I wanted to have sex with, so I'd never had to deal with the issue head-on. Now here I was with Braslav. We were just a few hours into our time together. As far as being cooped up in the cab together, well, we were only an hour out of Belgrade. The whole night lay ahead...

Braslav...

We ran through a station. Nedim dutifully reported it. 'Ruma,' he said. It had to be Ruma: there was no other place of any size between Belgrade and Vinkovci. That was Ruma all right, a few little lights gliding by in the dark. I didn't say this to him. I said, 'Thank you, Nedim,' instead.

I looked at my watch. Ten twenty-three. We were running just a few minutes late. Snow piling up on the rails in places was slowing us a bit. We'd left Belgrade on time at nine fifteen. We were due at Vinkovci at eleven fifty-eight. I wasn't surprised when, about fifteen minutes later, Nedim said in a rather shy tone of voice, 'This is a bit awkward. I think I need a piss.'

'Just do it on the coal,' I said. 'That's what I do. Don't you do that?'

'Not on the saddle-tanks,' he said. 'We don't do long runs. The question never comes up.'

'Well, suit yourself,' I said. 'But if I were you, I'd just do it. It's only you that's going to shovel it up.'

He giggled at that, turned towards the hatch from which the coal in the tender was spilling out onto the floor behind us and started to unbutton himself. I did something irresponsible at that point. I said, 'May as well follow your example,' turned and stood alongside him and started to get mine out.

Of course his penis was massive. It was circumcised, as those of his religion's sons usually are. Nevertheless, I didn't feel I had anything to be ashamed of. Unlike Nedim I wasn't big in stature, perhaps a little under average height, but I knew that my cock was a large one for someone of my size. Other men had told me that.

By the time we'd both finished and were shaking ourselves dry Nedim was beginning to stiffen up. I could see that he was embarrassed about it. 'Don't worry about that,' I said. 'It happens to all of us.' As if wanting to oblige with a practical example my cock suddenly did the same as his. 'You see?' I said. But it was perishing cold and we both stuffed them away with our mittened hands – albeit with a bit of difficulty – very quickly after that.

Nedim turned very quickly towards the glazed lookout porthole that faced forwards. 'I hope we haven't missed any signals,' he said with alarm in his voice.

'Don't worry,' I said. 'There aren't any hereabouts.'

Except the signals we'd been flying ourselves, I thought.

Nedim…

I hadn't expected that scene. There was a moment

afterwards when I thought I would have done better to say nothing and to have held on until either we reached Vinkovci or I wet myself. But then I thought that life was an extraordinary adventure. Being here on the Orient Express was an extraordinary part of it. Meeting Braslav was another part of it. What had happened (although nothing had happened I somehow felt that it had) seemed a pointer to something else: a possibility that hovered ahead of me, frightening yet appealing, awful but wonderful. Life was an adventure, I told myself. I had to accept that. Had to take what life had in store for me and make what I could of it.

We reached Vinkovci thirty minutes late. Only forty minutes before we were due at the next station, which was Brod. There was no way we could make up thirty minutes in that short time, even in the best of weather. And hour by hour, and as we climbed, the snow had been getting worse. The station master at Vinkovci telegraphed ahead to tell his counterpart at Brod we would be arriving late.

A very small number of people got off the train at Vinkovci, and an even smaller number got on it. The stationmaster and Braslav exchanged their very unequally matched whistles, Braslav opened up the regulator and slowly, solemnly, 72619 moved out of the lighted platform and into the swirling dark.

That noise of tearing silk. We were getting used to it. Again and again it came. The snow-slap against the cab side sounded each time more aggressive than the last. 'Drifting a bit,' said Braslav.

17

We had said goodbye to Serbia and were now in Braslav's homeland of Croatia. In daylight you could hardly tell the difference. Let alone in this.

We had also parted company with the Danube, and had forked into the tributary valley of the Sava. The Danube valley funnels the north wind down it. It blows straight across towards the Sava river. Towards Brod there are some low mountains in the wind's path. It ignores them, comes straight over the top and blows towards the Sava with increased force. It was blowing a north wind that night. It blew into the cab on Braslav's side, and blew out again on mine. We were both just as cold. Our ears tingled with the frost.

I was looking ahead through my small porthole. I suddenly felt Braslav's arm around my shoulder. 'Hey, mate,' he said. 'You need warming up.' And then to my astonishment I felt him tweak my ice-cold left ear and then fondle it. To my more than astonishment I responded by putting my arm around his shoulder and fondling his chilly right ear in my turn. In my wildest dreams I had never guessed that such a reflex was a part of me; had never imagined acting on such an impulse; had never expected I would behave like this.

Braslav turned me round to face him – we had to abandon each other's ears in order for this to happen. He said, 'Have a nip of this.'

In his other hand was a hip flask, the top already off. I said, 'I've never drunk alcohol. I'm not supposed to.'

He said, smiling very gently, 'No-one's ever going to find out.'

I thought of saying that, of course, God might. But then I asked myself if I really thought that. And how much did I really believe in God...? I took the hip flask from him and raised it to my lips. Whatever the liquid was, it felt as if I was drinking the fire from out of the firebox, but by heaven I could feel it doing me a power of good.

'Go easy,' I heard Braslav say. 'Especially if you're not used to it. It can have interesting effects.' I handed the flask back.

By now the sound of tearing silk was continuous, and the patter against the cab of the ice the wheels were churning had become a low menacing roar. So much slush was finding its way in under the partition that the cab floor was awash. Our progress was slowing noticeably. I piled more and more coal into the firebox, heaping it up with the vigour and strength that is given to people for a short time after they've had a quick strong drink. Braslav had the regulator fully open and the exhaust steam and smoke was flying high above the funnel into the night. Our way ahead, or what remained of it, was lit now by roaring flames and crackling sparks.

Or what remained of our way ahead... In a moment of awful shock I saw something in front of us that froze the alcohol in my veins. 'Shit, Braslav! You've got to brake. There's a wall of ice!'

Braslav leaped to his window, leaped back again, shut off the regulator and frantically slammed the brake. 'Christ almighty!' he said. I understood what he meant.

The tearing of silk crescendoed into something deafening. There began a terrifying juddering during which we rocked from side to side and I thought the engine would go over and we'd be crushed under it. But then the juddering stopped, the noise stopped, and we stopped. I was thrown forward towards my window and hit my head on the glass. Braslav nearly fell into the fire but saved himself. It was with horror that I watched this. There was an almighty silence that echoed so loudly in my head that it seemed to hurt. But we were still alive. 72619 was still upright. Braslav managed to smile at me as he picked himself up. But his smile didn't come easily. It was a smile that was intended to give me courage. I realised that. He was sharing with me what remained of his own stock of it. I blessed him for that.

The regulator was closed, the fire was piled up. With nowhere else to go now the steam made its pressured way out of the safety-valves just in front of our cab with a despairing whooshing sound. Once the valves had started to blow it seemed to me there was no way they would ever stop. There went the results of all my recent labour, belched out despairingly: un-reclaimable energy wasted, lost into the cold-hearted night. It seemed a metaphor for the futility of all human effort. I felt my shoulders start to heave, and to my shame, because I was in the presence of Braslav, I started to sob.

THREE

Braslav...

I knew he was going to hit his head. I saw it happening as if watching a cinema film in which they had slowed the action down. I saw myself reaching him in time, catching his forehead in my hands and taking the blow on the knuckles of my fingers, in his place. But I couldn't do that. I could only move at the slowest speed myself. It was like an awful dream in which I was trying to escape from something but could not summon my muscles to my command. With an almighty shock the compacted drift finally halted us. I was less than halfway towards Nedim – a distance, admittedly of a mere six feet. I fell forward onto the floor. Putting my hand out as I went down I found the fire-hole door handle and – in more ways than one – saved myself. The fire door slammed shut just in time and my shoulder slammed against it. I picked myself up at once, turning towards Nedim and managing, I hoped, to give him a grin of reassurance. He was looking at me. He looked thunderstruck. Blood was running from his forehead and, as from any head wound, it ran fast. He was trying not to cry.

There had been occasional moments in my life when it was given to me to understand exactly what was happening in a fellow human being's mind and heart. There hadn't been many, but this was one of them. It was the biggest yet. Nedim wasn't crying because he'd hurt his head or because we'd crashed. This trip on the Orient Express had been his dream – looking back I could see the signs of that – and now his dream lay shattered at his feet and exposed for the fragile bauble that it was.

Life returned to normal speed. I stood and moved towards him, pulling a handkerchief from the pocket of my boiler-suit. Holding it out I clapped it to his forehead. 'You're bleeding,' I said. My other arm went around his back of course. I couldn't help myself.

To my complete astonishment Nedim threw both his arms around me and kissed me, with a sweet taste of alcohol, on my lips.

'Schätzchen,' I said. Darling. It just slipped out. German was the first language of the Austro-Hungarian Empire, to which the Balkans had belonged till just a dozen years before. We still used it occasionally in moments of great importance, even if sometimes by accident.

'Schätzchen,' Nedim said. So softly that I might not have heard it, had he not pushed his great shoulders against my smaller ones and nuzzled his bleeding head against my neck. He started weeping then, and I found myself guiltily welcoming the mixture of sweat and tears and blood that was trickling onto me. But I welcomed them only because the blood and sweat and tears were part of *him*. It wouldn't have been the same if they'd come from anybody else. Softly I caressed the top and back of his head through his leather cap.

Nedim...

A muffled voice was calling. *'Zdravo!* Hallo there. Are you there? Are you all right? Are you hurt?' The voice came from behind the tender. The conductor had opened the connecting door – the one that had no door opposite it to connect with – and, shouting through a twelve-metre block of water, coal and steel, was trying to contact us.

We broke off our unexpected, earth-changing embrace, and I used Braslav's hanky to mop my face of tears and blood. It hadn't been clean when he gave it to me. I didn't mind that. It was full of him. Full of the scent, and more, of Braslav.

'We're OK,' Braslav shouted back. Then, to me, 'Can you climb up?' He looked at me as I held the hanky to my head. 'One-handed? Or shall I do it?'

'I'm taller,' I said. 'I'll go.'

There were iron cleats in the wall of the tender, next to the coal hatch, and I started to scramble one-handedly up. It was surprisingly easy. Why was it easy? The answer was easy too. I was doing it for Braslav.

As my head came up over the tender top I could see the front of the nearest carriage, eerily lit by the dim glow of a lamp. The lamp was presumably being held by the person I couldn't see, down in the gap between tender and carriage. The light didn't show me the roofs of the other carriages. The darkness and the blizzard saw to that. I shouted, 'We're all right. Are any passengers

23

hurt? Are all the carriages still attached?'

'Think so. We're still checking. I thought I should see about you, though. You bore the brunt of it. Whatever it was.'

'Snowdrift,' I said. I wasn't going to be over-dramatic, repeating what I'd said to Braslav in my moment of panic: that we were running into a wall of ice. 'I'm coming over the coal,' I said.

I scrambled up on top of the tender and, with some difficulty as I was still pressing the hanky against my head, half-walked, half-crawled my way across the jagged carbon heap. I had always admired the casual insouciance of three-legged dogs and cats and their refusal to give in to self pity. I thought of them now and just got on with it.

A moment or two later I was standing upright on the top of the water tank. Below me was the plan-view of a Wagons-Lits conductor's uniform peaked cap and solid shoulders with epaulettes. *'Zdravo,'* I greeted the top of the cap.

The cap tilted back and a foreshortened face looked up from underneath it. 'Thank God you're all right.' The face frowned a second. 'You the driver?'

'Fireman,' I said.

'The driver…?'

'Unhurt,' I said. My life had changed as dramatically

as if I'd fallen over a cliff. Maybe Braslav's also had. I couldn't know that yet. But at least we were both unhurt...

'You're not unhurt,' said the conductor in a concerned voice. 'Look at you... You're bleeding all over the place.'

'Head wounds do that. It's nothing. Skin-deep. I banged against the porthole when we hit.'

'We'll get you down here in a minute. Get you patched up. Must go and see to things my end. Back in five minutes, that's a promise.' The conductor began to turn to go back inside the carriage but a voice stopped him.

'Zdravo.' The voice came from right beside me. 'I'm the driver. Call me Braslav.'

The conductor turned back abruptly. 'Have you inspected the drift? Can we get through, do you think?'

'With a pair of shovels? You're joking. It's a solid wall of ice. Alongside the engine it's higher than the driving wheels. You can't step into it. It's as high as the top of the boiler a little way in front.' So Braslav had climbed out along the running-plate and edged his way forward to have a look. 'It'll need a snowplough and a team of men. We're stuck here for the night I should think.'

'Can we telegraph?'

'The poles are down. I doubt it. They'll know what's happened soon enough.' Braslav pulled out his pocket watch. 'We're already overdue at Brod.'

'Well, you can't stay in the cab in the freezing cold all night,' the conductor said. 'We'll sort you two lads out a bed.'

I supposed that was a slip of the tongue. Two lads, one bed? It's easy to get a detail wrong in Serbo-Croat.

'Thank God for that,' said Braslav. 'We need to sort the fire out first.'

'Come back over the coal when you're ready. Ask for me. My name's Sacha.' He looked hard at Braslav. 'You got a bandage box up there? Get your friend bandaged up.'

'Of course,' said Braslav, as hotly as he would have countered an insult. 'I haven't had a second…. Of course I'll do that.' I'd picked up on Sacha's choice of the word friend. It sounded as though Braslav had also picked up on it.

'Good,' said Sacha. 'I must see to my end of things. See you shortly.' He turned, went in through the door and pulled it to behind him, though without fastening it. Those connecting doors were not equipped with bells or knockers.

Braslav turned to me. 'How could I have? What was I thinking of?' He still spoke hotly, but now he sounded as though he was loathing himself.

26

'What?' I asked. I didn't understand him. I had no idea what he meant.

'Let you scramble over the coal while you were holding a rag to your face. I thought you'd just peer over the top and shout. Of course you didn't. It should have been obvious. I should have gone myself.'

'It isn't a rag,' I said almost equally vehemently. 'It's your handkerchief.'

Braslav...

I nearly fell apart when he said that. Me! Fall apart because of something some boy says about a handkerchief?! He went on, 'You had things to do. You wouldn't have sent me out to balance along the running plate to inspect the front of the loco, would you? Of course not. So you mustn't think like that.'

We were talking in a most intimate way, I realised. Not the way driver and fireman talk together but the way a man and his woman talk. I had never had a conversation like this with a man before. I took his arm to help him balance as we scrambled together back across the coal. Ahead of us, beyond the roof of the cab we saw the twin pillars of steam still rising with the energy of geysers from the safety-valves. 'What are we going to do with her?' I said. Normally I made those decisions myself. I would never have dreamt of asking my fireman's opinion before deciding something like that before tonight.

We discussed it like a pair of equals while I bandaged

Nedim's head. Once the fire had died down a bit we would keep it going overnight, well damped. Then it wouldn't take long to build it up and get steam back up when the plough arrived and released us in the morning. We would have to take it in turns to get up and check on it a couple of times during the night. We, I said. It was actually the fireman's responsibility, not mine, to do that. Did it cross my mind to mention the fact? I think you know the answer to that.

I couldn't help thinking ahead. Sacha had talked about a bed. A bed each was obviously what he meant. The conductors slept on couches in the corridors of the carriages they attended, so they could be called upon by any passenger who stuck their head out of a compartment door with a request for a bottle of water or a complaint about a draught. That was probably what Sacha would offer us. Probably we'd be at opposite ends of the train. We would be grateful for that. To lie down in the warm...

Sorry, I couldn't help it: I found my imagination had run ahead to something that was clearly impossible. A night in bed with Nedim. I found myself grinning sheepishly at the silly thought, and was glad Nedim was busy dealing with the damper levers so he couldn't see my face. I'd had sex with men in toilets. Not often, though it was still enough for me to feel guilty about it. It was something punishable by eternal torment, my Church had told me. Whether I still believed that I wasn't sure. But even to have been told that a few times in my early life was sobering enough. I only had to look through the fire-hole door into the infinite wrath of the firebox to be reminded of that.

But now the massive conflagration Nedim had conjured in the hope that we could power our way through the drift had passed its peak. It wasn't exactly dying down yet, but it would get no hotter. Everything that lay on the great fire-bed was well and truly alight. It would quieten down now, especially when, in a few minutes, Nedim pulled the damper levers shut. Above our heads I heard the safety valves lower the pitch of their shrill hisses. I smiled at Nedim. 'Hear that?' I said.

'Ah,' he said. 'The vipers are losing their teeth at last.' I thought suddenly that Nedim had a bit of a way with words, and felt proud, though quite unjustifiably, of having made a friend of someone who could say things like that. But then he surprised me yet again. He leaned towards me and gave me another kiss. Though this time only on the cheek. Then he chuckled and said, 'You know that hip-flask. I don't suppose…?' I laughed aloud at that and rumpled the top of his cap. And of course I did let him take another nip.

Nedim…

We clambered together across the coal again and helped each other down the back end of the tender. The blizzard now was less ferocious, but still the snow fell steadily. I had the feeling it would continue throughout the night. Light spilled out from under the not quite closed connecting door. We pushed it open and, like children entering a forbidden place crept quietly, awed by the experience. We found ourselves, by contrast with where we'd just been, in a realm of warmth and light. We fastened the door behind – to stop the warmth-light magic seeping out.

I had never been inside a carriage of the Orient Express. I was dumbstruck. I was walking in my oily boiler-suit and coal-grimed boots along a carpeted corridor that looked as though it belonged in a palace. Instinctively I doffed my cap. Braslav stopped my progress with a hand across my midriff as he stopped walking himself. 'I don't think it's our caps we need worry about,' he said. 'I've just thought, we ought to take our shoes off.' Feeling guiltily that we should have thought of this a few seconds earlier we now knelt down and did this.

While we were still kneeling the door at the end of the carriage ahead of us opened and Sacha came through it. He laughed when he saw us. 'Thank you for your thoughtfulness,' he said. He was a gentleman, was Sacha. By which I mean he didn't look past our shoulders for the evidence of our initial lack of thought.

'Welcome,' he said. 'We're in the Athens-Paris coach. There's almost nobody aboard it, though the rest of the train is packed. You can sleep in one of the compartments. They've two bunks each.' He paused and looked rather appraisingly at us. 'Unless you'd prefer a separate compartment each.'

Braslav spoke before I could. Almost too readily, I thought. 'One will do us fine,' he said. Did I see an amused smile begin to form on Sacha's face, a smile he quickly suppressed? 'Thank you,' I said.

'Then here you are,' Sacha said. He pulled open a door that was veneered in decoratively grained mahogany and showed us inside.

The space was not enormous. It was no less astonishing for that. A richly upholstered sofa, dove-grey, occupied one wall. Above it, and on the other walls were panels of veneer of mahogany and rosewood, inlaid with intricate marquetry designs in ebony and satinwood. An oil-lamp hung, in an elegant shade, from the roof. In the window another one stood. 'I'll show you how the beds are made up,' Sacha said. He pulled a lever and the sofa rearranged itself into a bunk bed, while from the ceiling dropped a second, upper bunk. With it came a ladder for ascending to the upper bed. 'I'll put it back the way it was, shall I?' Sacha asked. 'You'll probably want something to eat and drink first.'

Sacha raised a small mahogany shelf in the corner. It snapped satisfyingly into a brass catch. A beautiful porcelain wash basin lay hidden beneath it. Next to its two bright taps lay a tiny pristine bar of soap. An art deco bracket light overhung it. Sacha showed us a tiny hook on the wall just inside the door. A small circular pad of felt was fixed beneath it. 'For your driver's watch,' he said, and grinned shyly, hoping perhaps that Braslav wouldn't take offence at his joke. But Braslav took the joke and ran with it. He removed his steel watch from his pocket and hung it up. 'No sooner said than done,' he said.

Sacha said, 'The toilet's at the end of the corridor.' He frowned delicately. 'Try to keep it clean. Remember they're First-Class passengers you'll be sharing it with.'

I said, 'We'll do our best.'

Sacha looked me up and down, taking in my smoke-grimed, bandaged state. An indulgent look appeared on his face. 'I'm sure you will,' he said. 'But don't worry too much. An emergency is an emergency. Passengers, even First-Class passengers, understand that.'

Braslav said, 'We asked about the train, the passengers…'

'Rest assured,' Sacha said. 'All rolling stock intact. No passengers or conductors hurt. Most people were asleep in bed and few have woken up. You are the boys who took the brunt.' He paused for a second to marshal his thoughts. He went on, 'Another unexpected guest is sharing the carriage with you tonight, by the way. One of the Wagons Lits company directors.' He shrugged. 'Not that you need to know that. He isn't any different from the rest of us.' He paused again and shook his head. Then, 'Right, I shall go and fetch you sheets, towels and blankets. And something to eat. There's things left over from the passengers' dinner. Consommé. Turbot. Lamb cutlets. Frittered apricots. That all right?'

'Yes,' we both said, gibbering the word in our astonishment.

'To drink: champagne, Eau Perrier and coffee. Are you both OK with that?'

'Champagne's fine for me,' I blurted out stupidly. 'The only thing I don't do is pork.'

'Ah, Jewish,' said Sacha, smiling understandingly. 'And nothing wrong with that.'

I had no intention of putting him right.

FOUR

Braslav…

We barely waited to hear the click of the closing door before we were all over each other. It seemed to me that Nedim was far more sexually experienced where men were concerned than I was. He was quickly thrusting his tongue into my ear and exploring in there, as if he were practising for similar explorations of other parts of me, while we hugged, cuddled and fumbled each other through our thick coats. After a minute I pulled away, laughing, and said, 'Perhaps we should take our coats off at least.' Nedim saw the point of that and unfastened his at once, throwing it to the floor. He then started on his boiler-suit. I stopped him with a hand. 'What have you got on underneath?'

'Sweater, trousers, long-johns…'

'That's all right, then,' I said. 'It's just that Sacha will be back in a second and we ought not to be in our underwear when he arrives.'

'You mean you think we should be sitting here without it?' He burst out laughing at the brilliance of his joke. I realised that the few swigs of schnapps he'd taken had had a major impact. It was not to be wondered at, since he'd never tasted alcohol before and his system was quite unused to it. I made a mental note to be careful, when the champagne arrived, to monitor his intake and if necessary curtail it. For the moment we simply undid and pulled off each other's boiler-suit.

Before me stood a young man in a thick grey sweater, cable-knit; he had on a pair of chocolate corduroy trousers, and worn grey socks from which his two big toes peeped like plums. His shoulders were broad but he was slender at the waist and quite narrow at the hips. He had a head of hair that was thick, curly, shiny and black; a broad, Slavic forehead – like mine but on a slightly larger scale – and his eyes, beneath their gently arching brows, were almond-shaped and the colour of dark olives, framed with thick black lashes. His nose was squashy and his lips were sensuous and thick. His face was so dark with smuts and coal dust that you could think he'd made himself up with burnt cork like the minstrels do for the music halls. The bandage under his hairline added a piratical look. I had fallen for his looks the moment I first saw him, coming round the front of the engine at the depot. This view of him now sealed my fate.

I fell on him, my arms round his waist for the second time in minutes, and he returned my embrace with the kind of hug they say that bears give. A discreet knock at the door, however, caused us to spring apart. I called, 'Come in,' and Sacha entered, with towels and sheets, as he had promised. Then he ushered in a waiter with, not a tray but a trolley. The four of us plus the trolley entirely filled the small space. 'I won't disturb you again,' Sacha said. 'Just leave the trolley in the corridor when you've finished with it. And I'm sure your work will call you in the morning before I get round to it.' He glanced meaningfully towards the hook on the wall from which my watch hung splendidly. 'But if you need anything you'll find an attendant in the corridor of the next car.' The waiter bowed and left us, then Sacha too departed, though with a more man-to-man look.

Though I had never eaten like this, I did know that the soup came first, then the fish, then the meat and – well, everyone knows the dessert is last. I was glad too that I had uncorked champagne before – at family weddings. I would have hated to look foolish in front of Nedim.

Nedim…

It was like finding myself in a fairy tale. In one of Scheherazade's Thousand and One Arabian Nights. I was in a cave of treasures, filled with warmth and Lalique-framed light. After the freezing cold of the cab and our sickening experience in it this seemed like paradise.

This wasn't the big part of the fairytale; this was the easy bit. The other part was the shocking part: the part I didn't know how to deal with. It had a name at least; by now I knew that; its name was Braslav. When I took his boiler-suit off I found myself looking at a young man who was slim and wiry, a bit smaller than me, who had a mop of sandy curls, proud ginger eyebrows and ginger eyelashes. He had a broad Slavic forehead like I did, almond-shaped blue eyes and a cheeky nose that was squashy. Thick and sensual lips. I'd kissed them several times already: I knew all about those.

He looked a bit older than me. Probably because he was. By two or three years, I guessed. But also he looked a bit like me. If I'd had an elder brother, I thought, he might have looked like that. I had no way of knowing, though. I didn't have an elder brother.

Braslav expertly felt through the foil on the champagne bottle for something that would unloose it. I'd never seen this in real life. He twisted whatever it was, then twisted the bottle top and – abracadabra, there was a pop and foam came out from the top. It was a scene I'd only ever read about or seen at the kino... He poured me a glass of champagne. Before today I couldn't have imagined myself writing such a sentence. A glass of champagne... Me drinking champagne! Me drinking alcohol of any sort! But champagne on the evening of my first taste of the proscribed drink! And then, the subject of the sentence: he. He. The first really romantic evening of my life. And the other person was not she, as I had always supposed, expected and hoped, but he. He. It would take me some time and thought to make sense of that.

There was no doubt about one thing, though. I liked it. Whatever the consequences, whatever I might find myself feeling when morning came and we climbed across the frozen coal to tend the firebox, I liked this evening the way it was. I was liking it more and more. I was having the best evening of my life.

Braslav...

'You're crying again,' I said to him. I was hardly

37

surprised by it. I'd been crying too, though I'd tried to be careful not to let him see that. I was the older one, the senior one. I was also, in the context of our working relationship, his boss.

We'd had the best meal of our entire lives. I knew that went for both of us. The dishes had been kept warm on meths heaters for hours, we knew that. The consommé wasn't as hot as it might have been, but it was sitting in a beautiful dish with a silver ladle in it and a silver top... It was the best soup we'd ever had. The turbot was a bit dried at the edges but ... see above.

As far as the champagne was concerned I'd been as careful with Nedim's intake as I was with the cut-off wheel on the loco I drove. The cut-off fine-tuned the cylinders' firing. How much steam to put in and when – and what would result and when it would. I thought now that giving alcohol to someone who wasn't used to it was not unlike that. In the end it came down to instinct: you made a guess as to whether you'd got it right and hoped for the best.

'Nedim,' I said in a big-brotherly tone, 'You've had two glasses. I think that's about right. You know what happens to people who aren't used to drink...' He nodded submissively. 'Well, the effect it's having on you... I'll need to drink the rest of the bottle myself in order to catch you up. You can fill your glass with Perrier and drink that while you watch me finish it.'

That reads quite unpleasantly. But I haven't given you the context. We were sprawled side by side on the sofa.

Our trousers were down to our knees. Our two big cocks were pointing upward from our fork-angles and we were playing with each other's while they released copious streams of whatever it was called. Had anyone given the fluid a name yet? I didn't know. I'd seen it mentioned in none of the newspapers I read.

'You're right,' Nedim said, dreamily caressing my inner thigh with the hand that wasn't busy somewhere else. 'You have to be my teacher where alcohol's concerned. But champagne's special, isn't it? That taste, that fizz on the tongue, the buzz of it...'

'Nedim,' I said, 'have you ever sucked a man's cock?'

'No,' he said, and giggled.

'That taste, that fizz on the tongue, the buzz of it....'

He got my message. He leaned down into my lap.

Nedim...

Neither of us slept. We shared the lower bunk. We cuddled each other all night. I would pursue Braslav all the way to the wall in my desire to be close to him. I wanted to be with him, I wanted to be inside and outside of him, I wanted to be him. Then, when we'd reached the buffer-stop he would push me all the way back, till I was falling out of the bed and had to put my hand out to stop myself falling out. I'd call to him, 'Hey, Braslav, give me space,' and he would chuckle in his half sleep. He wanted to be inside and outside of me, he wanted to be me. I knew that. I knew that nobody had wanted me as much as this before. Certainly not the two girls I'd slept with in my random experiments. I knew that this was actually my first time. And – because insight is one of the things I'm good at – I knew it was a first for Braslav.

Braslav...

In the most perfectly imagined situation... Well, what would happen? I had no idea. That both men would come in each other's arseholes, first one, then, after a decent interval, the other? It didn't happen like that, of course. Why should reality bow to the power of my imagination, or Nedim's? Nedim sucked me for ages, yet, lovely though it was, I couldn't get there. When we'd got into bed we tried to fuck each other. Neither of us, it turned out, had fucked another fellow, and we lacked the technique. We both tried, yet failed, to penetrate each other. But our failure was a shared one. Our shame and humiliation would be our shared secret. We hugged the intimate knowledge of that failure together between us. As the oyster hugs its piece of grit. And the oyster's grit becomes in time a pearl. And our grit – in much less time – I think it took only till about four o'clock in the morning – became something I can find no word for – unless I dare call it love.

FIVE

Nedim…

It was wrong to sleep with another man in the way that a man sleeps with a woman. All my life I had been told that. I'd understood that and believed it. Part of me still thought that when I gave in to my desire for Braslav and climbed willingly with him into bed. But by the time day began to break the part of me that believed such a thing had grown smaller. By then a much bigger part of me was beginning to think the opposite: to dare to begin to believe that the rest of the world, and the whole of history since before the days of the Prophet, had got this wrong and that its was Braslav and I who were right. The reason for this? I knew by the time grey-fingered dawn was rendering the crystals that covered our bedroom window translucent, that Braslav and I were falling in love. It was just as well, it occurs to me now. We didn't know what the coming, terrible, day would have in store for us. Had we not been in the charmed, protected space that lovers occupy, I don't know how we would have got through it. As it was, even by the time of its dawning, I knew that today would be the most different and the most difficult day of my life to date.

Braslav…

The sun should have risen at about ten to seven. But this was to be a day on which the sun would never look, but turned away his face. Nedim, though, never turned away his face, but was all day turning to look at me, and that was, I think, the thing that got me through it. Even when, just before dawn, he began to doze off at last, one of his big arms round my shoulder, I felt that he was seeing me in his mind, gazing into my face through his sleep-closed eyelids.

I had to wake him up, though doing so hurt. I did it by stroking his ear-lobe gently, as my father had told me you had to if you wanted to wake someone without alarming them or making them cry out. At first my efforts had the effect only of making my lover rub his nose... (My lover? Can it be that I have actually written that?) ...but then at last he opened his eyes and they gazed steadily into mine, un-frightened, and I knew I had been right in guessing that he had been looking at me through closed lids all during the time, brief though it was, that he slept.

I said, 'Come, we must get up. We have to work.'

He got out of bed without complaint or comment and I admired him for that. We dressed, in the clothes we'd worn the day before: they were the only clothes we had with us. However, we watched each other as we did this and the sight, for both of us, was nice. For both of us? How did I know that went for Nedim as well as me? Because of the way he looked at me. Because of the smile on his face.

Nedim...

The windows on the north side of the train, the side

we looked out from in our compartment, were plastered with snow. They gave only a dim grey hint of light and we could get no impression from the inside of our sleeping-berth of what the outside world looked like. From the windows that looked out from the corridor, though, we could see a little more in the pre-dawn greyness, and once we had opened our compartment door and made our ways along the corridor to the toilet we spent a few minutes looking out. Putting off the moment, I suppose, when we had to return to our unshielded driver's cab and face there whatever we might have to face.

For now, protected by the cold plate-glass, we found ourselves gazing across an endless waste of white. The snow was falling only fitfully now and the wind seemed to have dropped. But clearly a lot of snow had fallen in the night and the wind had blown it about. It seemed to be nearly up to the running-boards on this, the lee side of the carriage. The depth of it on the other, windward, side we could only gloomily guess.

Dawn's dull lightness came grudgingly to us, in reflected form, from the snow, and it was even reflected from the low clouds above our heads. The clouds formed a seamless sheet, and the snow's reflection had turned the sheet a dirty, eerie bluish-white. We made our way along the corridor towards the door at the end, and as we neared the door I felt something tighten in the pit of my stomach like a rough knot.

The door didn't open. It was either frozen shut, or else the gap between the carriage and the tender had filled with blown snow, which was pressing up against it. After a few minutes of futile barging with our shoulders, we gave up on it and turned our attention to the door that was nearest it, the door from the corridor from which passengers would alight onto the platform. To my surprise this door opened after just one hefty push and, after no more than a second's hesitation, Braslav jumped out of it.

His legs disappeared up to their knees, but he was still standing well above the ground: the snow had compacted under his feet as he landed, and his face looked back at me from a height that was only a couple of feet lower than my own head. When he looked up at me he grinned unexpectedly. That gave me a feeling of courage, as well as filling my heart with all kinds of things that were more wonderful and complicated than that. I followed his example and jumped.

I'd seen hares and rabbits bouncing, half tunnelling, their way through deep snow, and that was how we travelled alongside the tender to reach our cab. Looking up at the gap between the tender and 'our' carriage we saw that it was indeed filled with driven snow. We hadn't been able to open that door because of it. When we got up to the cab we saw that the snow had melted alongside the locomotive as a result of the heat from the boiler and firebox and created a sort of water-filled moat about a foot wide. The water in it was ankle deep. At the front of the engine the snow hadn't melted so much, and the boiler door was still buried in the drift ahead of it. Buried up to the point where, if you'd wanted to paint a face on the front of the boiler, you'd have put the mouth.

We got down into the 'moat', then climbed the iron steps and stood on the footplate. It was wet but not snow-covered. Nor was the snow piled up on the other side of it. But it wasn't far distant. Just a foot away, at bay because of the fire's warmth, it reared up like a white wall. It was so high that we couldn't see over the top of it. It was a brooding, threatening presence, ready to encroach and to invade the cab if, or when, or as soon as, the fire went out.

I opened up the fire-hole door. The fire had lasted, thanks to our damping it, six hours through the night. Now it needed to be resurrected. Even if we weren't able to drive out of here today, the fire was needed to heat the train. There were small stoves in each carriage that took care of the water that passengers washed in, Braslav had told me, and a coal-fired stove in the kitchen that was attached to the restaurant car, but we still needed the engine's steam in the train's steam-pipes and brakes. In the awful event that we were marooned here for days, only our engine's fire would keep us and our passengers from freezing to death.

I opened up the dampers. I hardly needed to look at the chute of coal that tumbled from the tender hatch to know what had happened to it. To know what I would have to do with it. I reached for the pick-axe.

Simultaneously Braslav took hold of the long-handled hammer. 'You don't do that,' I told him. 'That's my job.'

He looked at me and smiled. 'Don't be a stupid boy,' he said softly. Then he leaned forward and gave me a kiss with the coldest pair of lips that had pressed against mine in my life.

Braslav...

I was worried about the safety-valves. Supposing they had frozen in the night and that, when the boiler reached pressure, they would refuse to work? As we broke coal together and Nedim shovelled it I watched the slowly rising pressure needles with apprehension. There was no point my worrying Nedim about this. I kept my anxiety to myself for the time being, but eventually I decided I would need to experiment. I had to tell Nedim now or he'd have got a shock. 'Going to test the whistle now,' I said. 'See if it works.'

'You mean, see if the safety-valves work,' said Nedim. 'I thought you might be worrying about that.'

'Why did you think that?' I asked him.

'Because I've been worried about it too,' he said. 'Didn't want to alarm you.'

I was already glad that I was working with Nedim rather than anybody else. But f I hadn't been, then that little conversation would have clinched it.

I pulled down on the whistle chain and heard a low rasp in the whistle's throat. It rose then into something like its usual scream. I let go of the chain, my limbs suddenly weak with relief. I turned to Nedim. 'It seems we're all right,' I said.

He said, 'I think we're in with a chance.'

We went back to splitting the frozen lumps of coal apart. My back began to ache. It was years since I'd done my brief stint as a fireman on the way up to the job I now had. I was out of practice with this. Were we going to have to spend the rest of the day doing this? I wondered. And the next day...? A chill of fear ran through me. Would we go on breaking coal like convicts in a stone quarry until ... until the coal ran out? I began to voice a question. 'Nedim, how long would it be, if we had to go on using the fire for heating only, before...?' But I was cut short by another voice.

'Zdravo. Zdravo.' Hallo up there. Nedim and I both dropped the tools we were using and moved to the side of the cab, leaning out through the glassless side lookout. Below us, up to his thighs in the snow on the other side of the moat, stood a large man in a dark blue Wagons-Lits uniform that had a large amount of gold braid on it. He was the *chef de train*, the boss of the conductor, Sacha, who had looked after us.

The *chef de train* bowed very slightly to us. 'I trust you passed a comfortable night, gentlemen,' he said.

'We were looked after very kindly, thank you,' I said. 'Sacha...'

'Yes, yes,' the chief conductor cut me off. 'I came to inspect the situation at the front. I can see with my own eyes that it isn't good. No job for just two men with shovels. I was informed ... I mean Monsieur Radmacher, your friend Sacha, told me ... the telegraph poles are down. There is no way I can think of for asking for help. Unless...' He looked away across the whiteness to the featureless horizon, then looked back at us with an un-readable expression on his face. 'Unless we walk.'

'Surely it won't come to that,' I said. 'They'll send a snowplough from Brod. It's only a few miles ahead of us.'

'And if they haven't got a snowplough at Brod?' the *chef de train* asked bleakly. 'And if the snow is like this all the way to Brod?'

I had no answer to that. I tried to visualise the sidings at Brod. Had I ever seen a plough sided there? I wasn't sure I had.

The chief conductor continued. 'Can we reverse back to Vinkovci? At least get the passengers off. Hotels. Food...'

I shook my head. 'There've been hours of snow and blizzard since we stuck in this. We've no snowplough on the back of the train. No heavy driving-wheels to pull us through it. We'd derail at the first drift. And I don't know if you've seen the other side of the train. The north side. The snow's nearly up to the carriage roofs.'

'So...?'

'We're doing the only thing we can do, for the moment,' said Nedim, jumping into the conversation suddenly and speaking with a confidence that surprised and impressed me. 'Making enough steam to heat the train behind us, and to be ready to move off as soon as rescue arrives and we're dug out.'

The *chef de train* looked at him. 'You are the fireman, I imagine,' he said. 'I have to ask you a grim question. How long, in your opinion, if the worst happened and we weren't rescued today or...' He stopped. I could sense he had a problem with the words *tomorrow* and *in the days ahead*. 'How long will stocks of coal and water last?'

It was the question I'd been in the middle of asking Nedim when the chief conductor arrived. Nedim paused a second before he gave his answer. Then he said, 'If we simply use the engine as a kettle for boiling water and damp the fire at night... then two days would be my rough guess.' His self-assurance departed and he looked at me for support. 'I've never worked on an engine this size,' he said. 'Am I right?'

I said, 'And I've never worked on an engine of this size or any other size in a predicament like this. Your guess is as good as mine. You're probably about right.'

'Thank you,' said the *chef de train*. 'The restaurant-car chef gave me a similar answer when I asked him what supplies of food we had. Two days, he told me. Two days of warmth and feasting...' He looked up at us very seriously. 'Two days and then what?'

'Rescue will come before two days are up,' I said.

'I'm sure of it.' Though I'd never been less sure of anything in my life.

'If it comes to rationing, then everyone will be treated equally,' said the chief conductor. 'Rest assured of that. In the meantime, have you breakfasted?'

We shook our heads. 'When you need to break from your labours come and look for M. Radmacher.' His lips twitched in a half-smile. 'Sacha to you. He has my authority to treat you as well as circumstances allow. This morning … some Balkan coffee and croissants I would hope, at the very least. Now I need to call the passengers to a meeting to give them the unpleasant news about our situation. We shall talk again later. I must get back.' He bowed slightly, turned and floundered through the deep snow in his sodden, once smart, uniform with as much dignity as he could summon up.

Nedim…

We did another hour's coal-breaking after the *chef de train* had returned to his duties. Then we heard the cheerful sounds of the safety-valves blowing a little, and knew that the fire could take care of itself for the short time it would take us to drink a coffee and eat a croissant. With some relief we realised also that the boiler was not going to blow up.

This time we hauled ourselves up on the tender again, the way we had done last night. But now we took shovels with us, and cleared a path through the deep snow on top of the coal and the water tank as we went. We shovelled the snow over the side of the tender. Then we tackled the drift that had formed like a wedge between the tender and the door that led into the corridor of our carriage. It was a tantalising job. We worked away from the top downward in the bitter cold, with hands that stung despite the gloves we wore, knowing that just inches away was a realm of light and warmth: a place with coffee and croissants in it. At least there would be for two days if it came to it. If it did come to it, then heaven help us after that, I thought.

Somehow we cleared the snow from around the doorway, only to realise that we'd closed it from the inside the previous night. We would have to climb round and return by the door in the side of the corridor from which we – and the *chef de train* too, presumably – had earlier come out.

But just as we were preparing to do this we heard the sound of someone on the inside unlocking the door and putting his shoulder to it. It swung open and Sacha stood in front of us. He looked pleased to see us, but there were signs of strain on his face.

'You must be frozen,' he said. 'Come and I'll find you some breakfast. I would have come out and brought you some coffee at least, but there have been developments aboard, and they've kept us all more than busy.'

'I'm sure they have,' I said to reassure him. 'We completely understand that.'

'You don't understand,' said Sacha. 'The development I'm talking about has been a terrible one. A nightmare in fact.'

'Yes?' queried Braslav, frowning.

Sacha dragged us inside and shut the door before answering in the relative comfort of the corridor, 'One of the passengers has been murdered in his bed.'

SIX

Braslav…

I felt a chill run down my back. A man had been murdered on a train that no-one could easily board or escape from. A corridor train. Within a hundred yards or so of the door behind which Nedim and I had spent the night. I was glad that Nedim was standing next to me when I heard the news. He was three years my junior but I suddenly found myself needing him, wanting his support. I'd known him less than twenty-four hours. How had this come about? 'God in Heaven!' I said. 'How did it happen? Have they caught the…?' I didn't know what word to use and my sentence fizzled out.

'It's very bad,' Sacha said. 'It happened in the night. Either just before or just after we hit the drift. No-one has left the train. How could they? It means the murderer is still among us.'

'Who…? How…?' Nedim had become as tongue-tied as I was.

'An American business-man,' said Sacha. 'Wounded many times with a knife.'

'What have they done with him?' Nedim asked.

'They've put him in the refrigerator truck along with the wine and what's left of the meat. Look, you must be freezing. I'll bring coffee to your compartment. I would ask you along to the restaurant car because in the extremity of our situation all protocols are suspended. But a detective is ensconced there, interviewing the passengers.'

'A detective?' I said, astonished. 'The police have reached the scene already?' I gestured out through the corridor window. 'Through this?!'

'No,' said Sacha. 'There's a private detective on board. He is known to the company director who shares this carriage with you. It is an amazing coincidence. M. Bouc has engaged his services on behalf of the Compagnie Internationale des Wagons-Lits.'

'An amazing coincidence indeed,' I said. 'A murder on the train and a detective on board to sort it out.'

'I suppose there was a doctor on board to examine the body?' said Nedim. A bit mischievously I thought, considering the circumstances.

'There is a doctor among the passengers,' said Sacha a little coolly. 'That's less of a coincidence. There is usually a doctor on board the Express. It's to do with something called the law of averages.' He opened the door to our compartment. 'Make yourselves at home. I'll bring you something to eat and drink.'

Home. The door opened, and the word opened, upon a whole world of ideas and thoughts that reflected off each other just as, now we entered our mirrored compartment, my reflection and Nedim's did.

Sometimes, when I had guiltily masturbated another man in a dirty toilet I had dared to wonder what that man's home was like. Did he live in cold and squalor? Was the place in which we now stood simply an extension of his ordinary existence? Was his home like this? Or did he have a nice warm house, with children and a wife?

Once or twice I'd found myself fantasising about a future in which I shared a life with another man. Shared a home with another man. I'd shut the thought stream off quickly each time, like a scalding tap. There was not the remotest possibility of such a thing coming to pass. Not in Croatia. Not, as far as I knew, in any country in the world. I couldn't even wait till I died and went to Heaven. There was no Heaven for men who liked other men's cocks. Unless we repented at the last minute we went to Hell instead.

So I had been told all my life. I considered myself lucky that I no longer entirely believed that. But the rest of it remained true. There was no home that I could share with Nedim anywhere on this earth.

And yet, and yet...

Here I was, embracing Nedim, now that Sacha had withdrawn and we had closed the door, in a place that had suddenly become home for us. Home with finely etched glass around the lights. Panelled walls of mahogany, rosewood and teak with marquetry inlay. Mirrors with elaborate frames of gilded plaster and wood. We had our wash-basin with its polished mahogany lid. We had our glowing lamps, we had our beds, we had our warmth. We had each other. We had our home already. We had us. I'd known Nedim less than a day – we were kissing now, pressing erections together through our overall trousers, and we had our hands up under our many layers of sweaters, shirts and undershirts – but already we shared a warmer, more opulent home than I'd dreamed of in my life. It was a home that would be ours for as long as... Bitter reality shrivelled the delicate blossoming of my thoughts. This would be ours only for as long as we remained stuck and marooned in this snowdrift.

Nedim...

Sacha knocked at the door discreetly and we sprang apart. Again he ushered in a waiter with a trolley. 'I would have brought the bacon and eggs the English like for breakfast,' Sacha said. 'But out of respect for the Jewish faith of one of you, which I remembered just in time...'

I was astonished. Braslav had told me he was Catholic. Then I remembered Sacha's misunderstanding of last night. I hadn't corrected him. Now I thought the time had come for this. 'I'm not Jewish,' I said. 'Call me Nedim. I'm of the Muslim faith.'

'It makes no difference,' said Sacha smoothly. 'We are all journeying towards the same truth, although from different directions. Just as all the railway lines of Europe converge on Trieste. But for that reason – I mean the matter of respect for faith – I have brought you poached eggs on toast with some smoked trout...'

And the coffee he had brought us was laced with brandy. I wouldn't have known this, though I thought it tasted a bit different. It was only after I'd finished it that Braslav, grinning shyly, pointed it out. After this breakfast from heaven, and no doubt encouraged by the brandy, I was ready to get into bed with Braslav and complete our unfinished business of last night. He wouldn't let us. 'We have work to do,' he said. He kissed me and buttoned me up, and then we left our haven of comfort and cosiness and opened the door behind the tender, climbed once more across the icy top of it and went on splitting the frozen coal lumps.

We worked mostly in silence, and in an extraordinary mixture of temperatures: with the fire-hole door open the fronts of us roasted like meat skewered on a spit; the rest of our bodies meanwhile nearly froze as cold as the snow that towered around and threatened to engulf us. But I wanted to say something to Braslav. It took the form of a question. I thought I couldn't bring myself to utter it. But, heated by the brandy in the coffee, it seethed away like the boiler in front of us and eventually some safety valve inside me reached the limit of its tolerance and blew my question out. It seemed to condense and freeze in the cold air that surrounded us. 'Braslav, what do you think is going to happen to us?'

The pick-axe he was holding fell dead in front of him and split the coal at his feet as if by accident. It was as if he, not just the pick-axe, had fallen dead. He looked at me with the expression on his face that he might have worn if he had just seen a ghost. 'What do you mean, happen to us? When are you talking about? Tonight? Tomorrow? For the rest of our lives? After we are dead?'

I hadn't put Braslav down as a deep thinker. But it was clear now that he'd been giving a lot of thought to this while I had not. My thoughts faltered and so did my voice. 'I don't know, Braslav. Tell me what you know about people like me... People like us. Tell me all of it.'

Braslav...

I didn't know what to say to him. I had no knowledge that wasn't negative. People like us were routinely cast away by their families if they were foolhardy enough to expose their inner selves. They were disinherited at the very least. At worst they were set on in dark streets, lynched, shot, or tortured, or doused with petrol and torched to death. 'I don't know what to tell you,' I said. And, as so often when I was faced with a question I didn't want to answer or else couldn't, I retorted with another question. 'Nedim, are you married?' I said.

I was braced and ready for either of his two possible answers. I wasn't prepared for the one he did give me, though, and it caught me under the diaphragm like a bayonet. 'Not yet,' he said.

'Not yet?' Perhaps because I'd been exerting myself breaking frozen fuel apart my words came out like a gasp. 'What do you mean? Are you engaged? What?'

'I'm not engaged,' he said. 'My parents expected me

to marry. That's all I meant. And in Bosnia we all marry. All men marry. Or become outcasts. So I will get married.' He shrugged his shoulders in a way that was less suggestive of stoic resignation, though, than of fury at his fate.

I said, and I tried to make my voice gentle, hiding my own rage at the way that society was set up, 'It isn't different in Croatia. It makes no difference if you're a Muslim or a Catholic. And for that matter it'd make no difference if we were Serbian and Orthodox, or homeless wandering Jews or Gypsies. "The foxes have their holes and the birds of the air have their nests, but men who love men have nowhere to lay their heads."' I realised with astonishment that I'd invented the last part of that. I'd never done such a thing in my life. 'Sorry,' I said. 'I think I made the last bit up.'

'You said love,' said Nedim. 'You said men who love men.'

'Yes,' I said. I knew as I said it that I was saying yes to something very big. I just wasn't quite sure what that big thing was. At least not in every detail. I knew the outline though. I was saying yes to Nedim. I was saying yes to Nedim and myself. I was saying yes to everything that life might bung at us.

Last night I had called him *Schätzchen.* Darling. Now suddenly I felt myself inhaling, gulping air and filling my lungs up as if I'd become an actor and was about to declaim an enormous speech. I felt my chest expanding, full to bursting, like an engine boiler just before the safety-valve went off. And then, as if the valve had blown suddenly, it ripped out of me. 'I love you, Nedim,' I said.

Nedim…

I hadn't manoeuvred him into saying that. Honestly, I had not. He had uttered the word love. My question had been a general one. It was about the feelings that men could have for other men: whether he thought they could amount to something as big as love. But he had gone two steps further at least. He had answered, not that he thought they could, or that he knew some who did, but that *he* loved *me*.

No-one had ever said that to me before, except my parents. Perhaps if I'd had brothers or sisters they might have done, but I didn't have any. Now I had no time to think how I might reply carefully. I needed to think very quickly and tell him, within the space of about a second, the honest truth, whatever that truth was. Images of everything that had happened between us flickered through my mind, like the cards that flicked past when you turned a handle and the still pictures joined together to make a moving one…

…A man came into view, walking round the front of the engine from the other side, clad in overalls like I was. We stared into each other's faces. Something happened at that moment. I didn't know what it was. I had the impression of a lightning flash…

…Braslav got out onto the platform to check the

attachment. I began to heap the fire up. Braslav climbed back in. 'Cold night ahead of us,' he said. 'You going to be warm enough?' He smiled at me in a way I found unusual. I was unexpectedly touched by that...

...I stopped shovelling and grinned my moment's exhilaration across at Braslav. To my surprise he was looking directly at me. Our two grins met, then grew together. I knew at that moment that something extraordinary had happened; I just didn't know what it was...

...Braslav managed to smile at me as he picked himself up. But his smile didn't come easily. It was a smile that was intended to give me courage. I realised that. He was sharing with me what remained of his own stock of it...

...Neither of us slept. We shared the lower bunk. We cuddled each other all night. I wanted to be with him, I wanted to be inside and outside of him, I wanted to be him. He would chuckle in his half sleep. He wanted to be inside and outside of me, he wanted to be me...

It took less than a second to run all that through my head. Then my answer came without doubt or hesitation. It came leaping out of me like a fish leaping from a deep lake. 'I love you, Braslav,' I said.

Braslav...

I had never dared to hope for so much from life. Here, in a freezing, open-to-the-elements locomotive cab, I stood in the greatest discomfort, chilled and running with quickly cooling sweat. I had just declared my love to a young man. That was one half of the great wonder of it. The other half, but by far the greater half, was that the young man, whom I found beautiful, sweet and good, had declared his love to me too. He was the first person in the world who had ever done that.

I pulled him towards me, muffled up against the cold as we both were, and kissed his lips. Then he said, 'But you haven't answered my first question. What is going to happen to us?'

'My darling darling,' I answered him, 'I may be three years older than you are, but you mustn't expect me to know the answer to that.'

'Perhaps love itself will take care of us,' he said, though there was uncertainty now in his voice.

'Perhaps it had better do,' I said, suddenly afraid, terrified of what the future might hold for us. That we were lost in the snow, our stocks of fuel and food quickly running out, that we might perish here in the train in this drift, seemed now only the beginning of our troubles. 'Love better take care of us,' I repeated. 'We've not much else.'

SEVEN

Braslav...

The kitchen staff found empty boxes from the food stores and broke them down into pathetically small planks which became duckboards or stepping-stones alongside the tender, creating a path along which they and the conductors, and we ourselves, could walk. The pathway was a necessity for a number of reasons. The coal was so depleted now that it lay low inside the tender, and it was no longer easy to climb over the top of it. Also, there was a need for small pieces of coal all along the train, to keep alight the small stoves that heated the water the passengers used for washing. And there was a bigger coal-fired stove in the kitchen attached to the restaurant car, which again had to be kept alight in order to provide hot food and drink.

I've mentioned drink and I've mentioned water. Coal was not the only thing that was running out. Of course we were surrounded by water, surrounded by endless fields of it. But it was in a solid state. We – Nedim and I, Sacha and his fellow conductors, the kitchen and waiting staff – scooped up buckets of snow endlessly. It takes no time at all to scoop up a bucketful of snow, but when you've melted it (we did this in front of the fire-hole door, the others used the top of the kitchen stove and the little stoves in the corners of the corridors in the carriages) there is very little water in the bucket. Fresh snow occupies a deceptively large amount of space.

As the day wore on the collection of water took over from the breaking of coal as our number one work priority. The conductors were trying to keep replenished the water tanks in the roofs of their carriages. By now this water was having to be hand-pumped. The kitchens also had a need for the precious liquid. Enough for cooking and making tea and coffee, and also for doing the washing-up. But it was Nedim and I who needed water most. We had a tank that held thousands of gallons. We couldn't possibly fill it up. The most we could do, by climbing the cleats at the back of the tender and tipping our buckets down the hole into the tank, was to try and stop the boiler running dry before the coal ran out. We worked at this like slaves, or like Hercules when he was carrying out one of his more impossible tasks. At least we were not trying to power the train with steam: we weren't going to drive it; we were just using the boiler like a kettle, to keep the train heated. The fire burnt slow and steady. We were also lucky in that the snow had stopped, and the coal we were using to put on the fire was not so frozen together as the morning's lumps had been. It was easier and quicker to break up.

We came in from the cold two more times during the hours of daylight, managing to warm ourselves for a few minutes each time in the beautiful compartment where we'd slept, and to where Sacha arranged on each occasion to send coffee and a sandwich. On both occasions the food and drink were delivered by the same young man who had served us breakfast in the morning and dinner last night. On the second occasion this young man had news for us. 'The detective continues to interview the passengers in the restaurant car,' he said. 'Though he did break for lunch. I hope he will have finished before dinner time, as we need to re-set the tables.' Then a thought appeared to strike him, as he frowned suddenly. 'But if he does finish, that will mean he has identified the murderer. What will we do then with a murderer on the train before the arrival of the police?'

'Best to cross that bridge when we come to it,' I said, though like the youth I found the thought an alarming one.

'But I have other news for you,' he came back unexpectedly. 'The *chef de train* has noticed that you have more work, and harder work, to do than anybody else. And so, while you are emptying buckets into the tender, he has released me from my other duties between now and dinner, to help you do it.'

'You?' I couldn't help saying. 'Unused to manual work. And dressed like you are...'

'I may not be big,' the youth replied, sounding a bit affronted, 'but I'm tough. My father has a farm and I have worked on it since I was a child. Also there are outdoor clothes and boots in the store. They are kept there for emergencies such as this. I will change as soon as I have removed your coffee cups. My name is Andrea, by the way. I come from near Trieste.'

Nedim...

I noticed then that Andrea was extremely beautiful. I

couldn't help it. I think I was at that stage of being in love, in first love's full flush, during which the beauty of other people seems somehow intensified, as the beauty of the world is intensified at the miraculous moment of sunrise. Yet somehow one is content to look and enjoy, without wanting to take and possess. Because one's cup is already overflowing and one has enough.

But I was not so taken with Andrea's beauty as to fail to remark something else. When Andrea said, just tossing the information casually out, that he came from Trieste, I remembered the last time I'd heard that place mentioned. Sacha had said, when trying to find a comparison for the idea that there were many equally valid paths to God, that all the railway lines of Europe converged on Trieste. I'd thought at the time that it was a strange place to pluck from the air. Why not Paris, or Berlin? Why had the familiar phrase *All roads lead to Rome* not come to his lips at once? Now, hearing Andrea tell us where he came from it crossed my mind that Andrea's place of residence had something to do with Sacha's surprising choice. I dismissed the idea at once, though. It was too fanciful, even for me. Far more likely was the fact that Trieste was the train's next big stop. Country border. Change of driver and fireman and locomotive. That was surely it.

Andrea was as good as his word. Within minutes of the end of our break he had joined us in the cab, climbing confidently up the iron steps, clad in a greatcoat and leggings, with leather boots and gloves and a felt hat. I was glad I'd already had a chance to observe his beauty, because if I'd first met him dressed as he now was I would have totally overlooked it.

We got a system going. Andrea went round the outside of the engine and filled two buckets, cramming the snow down inside with a small shovel as best he could. He handed them up to me on the footplate. I hung them on a long pole and pushed them inside the firebox for the half minute it took them to melt, then after wrapping the hot metal handles in rags I handed them back down to Andrea, who walked along the duckboards to the far end of the tender and handed them up to Braslav, who was perched on top. After Braslav had emptied the buckets he handed them down again and Andrea refilled them on the way back.

We quickly refined our routine. We used two sets of buckets, so no-one had to wait for anybody else. We spelled each other off. The person on top of the tender quickly got colder than the one inside the cab or the one who was walking around scooping snow up. It turned out not to be beyond the capabilities of Andrea to shovel an occasional ration of coal into the firebox once I'd shown him how to do it. Braslav didn't need showing, of course: he'd been a fireman before he became a driver. And so, by changing places every ten minutes by Braslav's watch (he was a meticulous timekeeper) we shared the work and the minutes in the warmth of the cab in a way that was equal and fair to all of us.

One time when Braslav and I were swapping places, passing each other on the duckboard path through the snow beside the tender, Braslav quickly embraced me and, thinking Andrea could not see us, kissed my lips. But at that moment Andrea popped his head through the cab lookout and spotted us. I was facing the cab, and saw this. Braslav, facing the other way, did not. Although Andrea's head disappeared back inside the cab as quickly as if someone had poured boiling oil on him from above, I thought it best to warn Braslav.

'Well, if he wants to make a fuss about it, we'll cross the bridge when we come to it,' was Braslav's response.

'The uncrossed bridges are mounting up,' I said, smiling. 'But somehow I don't think he's going to tell anyone, or make a fuss about it.'

'No,' said Braslav, investing the word with some significance. 'Neither do I.' I wondered if Braslav had had the same thought that I had had about Trieste. A second later there was a loud clatter of shovels from inside the cab and Andrea came backwards and quite noisily down the steps, trying to whistle a tune through his teeth.

Braslav...

We kept it up for two solid hours. It was bruisingly hard work. I learnt that day that hard work is not measured solely by its impact on your muscles and the time it takes up. It becomes harder or easier depending on the way you feel about it and because of the people you are working with.

I was already prepared to work twice as hard as I'd ever done in my life because of Nedim. Nedim working alongside me and inspiring me by his solid muscular presence. Three years younger than me. Bigger, more muscular. If I'm honest I have to admit that I felt obliged to compete and keep up.

But now as well as Nedim there was Andrea working with us. I guessed he was six or seven years younger than Nedim, so eight or nine years younger than I was. And because of that, but only because of that, I began to worry about Nedim. I began to worry about the impact that meeting Andrea might have on the man with whom I'd fallen in love.

I need to repeat that Nedim had fallen in love with me in the space of twenty-four hours, and that in the same space of time I had fallen in love with him. It happens in situations of extreme danger or tension or other seriousness. He'd fallen in love with someone three years older than himself. But how easily that could change, I thought. Love loves to wander, as Schubert tells us, and so I had a terrifying vision suddenly of Nedim transferring his recently awakened affections from me to Andrea. I knew more about the difficult things of life than Nedim did. The sudden arrival of Andrea on the scene of my thirty-six-hour-old relationship with Nedim was unsettling. I had watched Andrea closely during the two hours we'd all worked together. I'd seen the way he looked at Nedim. And occasionally at me. I was fairly certain that Andrea was… I don't know which expression I should use here. I'll settle for this one. *One of us.*

Nedim…

The moment came, of course, when Andrea would say something. All three of us could feel the imminence of this. We were like three safety-valves ready to blow. And when it did happen it happened like this.

It was getting dark. Actually it was already dark. Sunset was half an hour past. But the blue light reflected from the snowfields was giving us a few extra minutes of visibility in the flaky light of dusk.

Sacha strode into view along the duckboard path. He looked younger and more relaxed than he'd done when we'd seen him before. 'I need to claim Andrea back in ten minutes,' he said. 'The restaurant is clear. Andrea's team needs to lay up.' Then Sacha turned and walked back across the blue snow and was swallowed by the dusk.

It's funny how you remember, when important things are said, just where you were and how you stood or sat. So here it is. Andrea was crouched on the tender top. Braslav had told me to climb up and tell him to go, while he, Braslav, stoked the fire in a curious reversal of our official roles. As soon as my head arrived above the top of the tender and I saw Andrea looking down at me, the outline of his head and shoulders pinned on the darkening blue behind and above him, Andrea spoke.

'I know how it is with you and Braslav,' he said. 'I saw the two of you by accident. You know that. You saw me see you and I saw that…'

This could have gone on for ever and it was getting cold. 'Thank you,' I said. 'Your discretion…'

'That's not the point,' said Andrea, suddenly cross. 'I wanted to tell you something…' His voice lost confidence.

'Come down,' I said.

'The tank-top cap…'

'Leave it off,' I said. 'I'll sort it later.'

'I'll climb down the cleats…'

'No need,' I said. 'I'll catch you. Just jump.'

He did. I was touched beyond belief by his confidence in me. I would like to say that confidence was not misplaced. He was small and I was big and I was sure I would catch him easily and still stand up. But I did not. The duckboards collapsed under our combined weight and we went sprawling together in the deep snow.

Neither of us intended to wrap arms around each other as we struggled to stand up. It just happened. But that wasn't the important thing. The important thing was what Andrea said. 'I understand about you and Braslav. That you belong to him. It's the same with me and Sacha. I belong to him. Vice versa of course.'

'You're right,' I said. I was surprised at the growl that had become of my voice. 'It's like that. I belong to Braslav and he belongs to me.'

By now we were standing awkwardly on the snow, teetering on the brink of falling down again and holding each other up with the delicate mechanics of a hug.

I heard Braslav's voice. 'You two OK?' Looking up I saw him above us, peering down from the cab lookout.

'Belonging isn't easy,' Andrea said. I felt his hand around my back, now cupping one of my buttocks.

'I know,' I said. I was lying. I knew much less about belonging than Andrea did. But I had a go. 'I know it isn't easy. You have to work at it.' Those words just came out. I had no experience of any of this.

'I have to go and work now,' Andrea said, detaching himself.

He had to go and work?! As if two hours of shovelling snow and fuelling a steam engine and filling a sea-sized water tank wasn't work... Everything was relative, I supposed. But the idea that what Andrea had just been doing had made a holiday from his work in the restaurant car gave me pause for thought.

EIGHT

Braslav...

The first thing to fail was the toilets. They froze. From the bottoms up. Drifted snow had collected beneath the carriages and got into the outlet pipes. The flushes were still working that first afternoon, though, and the First-Class passengers used them without thought, until the toilets overflowed and covered the toilet floors with their piss and shit. That is what Sacha told us.

Nedim and I abandoned the toilet in the carriage we shared with the director of the Compagnie, the man who had employed the private detective. We trod out into the snow when the need presented itself, taking a roll of toilet paper with us. I had always taken a dim view of those unknown people who left bundles of used toilet paper strewn in the countryside. Now I had joined their number. So had Nedim. And, I guessed, also the Compagnie director. Needs must.

Presumably the other passengers were having to do the same. Men, whether first or second or third class, are used to this. But I felt sorry for the ladies.

Nedim...

When it got dark we came inside for a break. Sacha spoke to us. It was obvious from the way he talked to us this time that Andrea had told him about us and that he knew that Andrea had told him about Braslav and me...

I'm getting as bad as Andrea here. All was out in the open was what I meant. Though none of us referred to it at this point.

'It is inconceivable that rescue will not arrive tonight,' Sacha said. 'Or tomorrow morning at the very latest. After all, we are barely two dozen miles from Brod. So we are serving a full dinner tonight. Soup, fish, meat, cheese and dessert. Champagne, wine and port. I would like to invite you both to join the passengers in the restaurant car but…'

'It's all right, Sacha,' Braslav said gently. 'You don't need to tell us we're not dressed right. The passengers wouldn't be ready for that yet.'

'But maybe by tomorrow night…' I said. I meant to be light and flippant but I could see from the others' faces that my joke hadn't worked.

Sacha went back to frozen mode. 'There's no question of tomorrow night. We won't be here. This evening we'll bring you dinner in your compartment.' He thawed suddenly. 'In about two hours' time. Andrea will bring it. Wine included. With the Compagnie's compliments.' He looked at me and his face twinkled suddenly. 'I think even you will have no objection to a glass of wine. Given the exceptional circumstances.'

'Given the exceptional circumstances,' I said gravely. But Sacha knew that behind my poker face I had shared something with him that was deep and intimate.

Then Sacha said, to both of us, 'Can I ask a favour of

you? Before dinner. It's rather big, though. Could you manage to get a fire going beneath even one of the toilets on the train, to thaw it out and unblock it?'

We weren't going to say no. We were all in this. We went back to the engine and filled a bucket with live coals from the firebox. The restaurant chef stepped out from the restaurant car with wood from more empty vegetable crates. The three of us shovelled snow from under the end of one of the carriages – we chose a carriage that was centrally placed – and we managed to locate the outflow from the toilet. We built our fire beneath it…

Braslav…

We should have thought. Nedim was reaching across the fire beneath the carriage, putting more wood on it, when the toilet above him suddenly unfroze, unblocked, and disgorged its stowed load upon his shoulders and head.

Nedim was disproportionately upset, I thought at first. Dirt is only dirt, after all, and can be cleaned off. Then I realised that I was involved in this. Nedim was upset most of all because I was there to witness his humiliation, to see him in this state. At least the chef had gone back to his kitchen now: he wasn't here to witness this. Nedim crawled his scrabbling way back to me from under the carriage. He was swearing and crying by turns. I put my arms around his waist. Not around his shoulders or neck, I have to confess.

There were no baths or showers on the Orient Express. And our wash-basin, even if it hadn't frozen solid yet, would not be up to this. 'Drastic events need drastic solutions,' I said. Then, before Nedim had time to tense his big muscles or protest, I threw him down into the snow and rolled him in it. I rolled him round twice, then scooped the dirty snow off his shoulders and out of his hair with my hands. And then we both rolled one more time in clean snow to rinse ourselves off. After that we stood up very quickly. 'Get back inside,' I said. 'Get warm. You deserve a medal for this.'

'So do you,' he said.

We made our way back into our compartment. It had become our sanctuary from the world. It was the more precious for the fact that we would only have it for a few more hours at most. Now Nedim threw his arms around me, while we still stood in our soaking wet, though no longer dirty, coats. 'Thank you,' he said. He sounded very choked.

Something my father had once said came to me then. I told Nedim at once. 'If you are ever asking yourself whether you are in love or not, ask yourself this. Suppose the object of your affection shits themselves and needs to be cleaned up, would you do it?'

'I didn't shit myself,' Nedim objected frostily.

'It makes no difference,' I said, trying not to laugh. 'I still had to clean you up. And I'd have done the same if you had shat yourself. And I will do. When or if.'

Nedim's frostiness disappeared in an instant. I felt the thaw of him in his arms and face as he held and nuzzled me. He said, 'I'd do the same for you, of course. I don't need to tell you that, though, I'd have thought.'

I just held him for a second. Then I said, 'No, you didn't need to tell me that.' I don't need to write the next things that we said and did.

Nedim…

I hardly know how to describe that evening. I shall do my best. I'll leave out what happened when we were lighting a fire beneath one of the carriages to unblock the toilet, though. It wasn't very nice. Enough to say that Braslav told me something his father had once told him. It was a bit rough and ready, but there was a big truth in it. The funny thing was that my own father had once told me exactly the same thing. Later I told Braslav. He seemed surprised. But I suggested that perhaps it was something all fathers said, something passed down from generation to generation and he thought about that for a moment, then nodded his head.

We were never exactly off duty during this emergency. The fire needed tending from time to time, though we were keeping it very low now. We intended, if we were not rescued later in the evening, to damp it down overnight again. If the worst came to the worst and we were not rescued in the morning we would be able to heat the train till about midday. By then the coal would have run out. What would happen after that, if we hadn't been rescued by then was almost too awful to think about. Braslav and I didn't broach the subject. It was another of Braslav's bridges to be crossed when and if we came to it, I thought.

At least, thanks to Andrea's help, we had enough water in the tender to last the night.

It was warm in our compartment when we went in there at dinner time. Warm, thanks to our own efforts. Knowing that our dinner would be served by either Andrea or Sacha we took advantage of the warmth and stripped down to our Manchester cord trousers, removing shirts, vests, shoes and socks. Was that naughty of us, or provocative? I only knew, as I looked across at Braslav's lean pectoral muscles and his flat belly and his manly biceps, that this was nice. Braslav wasn't as big as me, but he looked like me in a slightly smaller size. I have to confess that I liked that.

Andrea arrived with our trolley. Sacha didn't accompany him. I saw Andrea's eyes widen as he looked at us. 'You two look nice,' he said a bit awkwardly. Then he relaxed. 'Enjoy your evening. And your night.'

I caught Andrea by the wrist as he unloaded the plates. Unwisely I asked him, 'Where do you two sleep?'

Andrea pulled away from my grasp. 'Sacha sleeps on the couch in the corridor of the next coach. I am restaurant staff. We sleep in hammocks stretched across the restaurant car after the passengers have gone to bed. We lash up and stow before the passengers wake.' He glared at me. 'You're not the only ones who lead a tough life.'

Braslav intervened on my behalf. 'We didn't mean to give offence. But you mentioned the restaurant car. The detective…?'

I could see that Andrea was a glad of a change of subject. So was I. I could feel my scalp prickling with hot embarrassment. Andrea said, 'The detective finished his work at five o'clock. His conclusion was that there was no conclusion. Because of the snow he narrowed his search down to the occupants of the carriage in which the murder happened. Apparently no-one passed into or out of the carriage during the whole night. He's exonerated all the suspects.'

'And so?' I couldn't help but ask.

'Presumably someone came into the train after we stopped, carried out the murder and then left. The driving snow would have covered his footprints.'

'Well,' said Braslav, sounding a bit disappointed. 'I think even I could have come to a conclusion like that. It hardly needs a detective to tell us that.'

I said, quoting Shakespeare, '"There's ne'er a villain dwelling in all Denmark but he's an arrant knave." "There needs no ghost, my lord, come from the grave, to tell us this."' I happened to have read Hamlet. Sometimes I couldn't resist showing off the fact.

Neither Braslav nor Andrea acknowledged my

moment of cleverness. Andrea bowed out of the compartment with his trolley and, left alone with Brslav, I felt my shame return. 'Should I apologise to Andrea when I next see him?' I asked

Braslav sighed, then smiled. 'No,' he said. 'When you have piled the fire too high there is no point adding more coal to it.'

Because of my exhaustion after the day's trials in the cold I fell apart. I broke down in tears and could say nothing. Braslav, who was sitting next to me on our upholstered seat, lunged around me and enveloped me with a hug. We were naked above the waist. The hug was hot skin on hot skin. I'd had too little experience of this, I realised. I knew now that I would want more of it, and would never be able to have enough.

'That wasn't a criticism,' I heard Braslav saying. 'It was just a comment. Forget it. For me you're simply perfect.'

Braslav probably meant to try to stop me crying. Actually his intervention had the opposite effect.

Braslav...

I wrote this on a paper serviette. I might not have remembered otherwise, and I wasn't sure I would ever eat like this again.

Iced melon with Marsala wine

River trout grilled in butter

Chicken baked in breadcrumb batter

Saddle of lamb, salt-marsh grazed

Asparagus tips in cream

Duckling in liqueur-flavoured aspic

Salad of aubergine and tomatoes

Cheeseboard

Soufflé with aniseed and kirsch.

It was all there on the trolley. Nedim and I scoffed the lot.

Nedim…

I drank champagne again. And claret. And burgundy. And port. After the meal I stood up and said it was my duty to bed the firebox down for the night. Braslav stood up too. He wasn't going to let me do it on my own, he said. Together, then, we stumbled around the side of the tender, stoked the fire, put the dampers on, and put 72619 to bed for the night.

Then we put ourselves to bed for the night. Got undressed like a couple who've known each other for ever and, like last night, tumbled together into the bottom bunk. 'Your teeth are chattering,' Braslav said as we wrapped arms around shoulders beneath the sheets and blankets.

'Sorry,' I said. 'I'm not cold. It's just…'

Braslav's arms, already tight around me, now gripped me like a vice. 'I know,' he said. And then his voice collapsed under the weight of everything he wanted to say but suddenly couldn't. 'It's the same for me.' It was hardly a sentence. More like a breath. Tear-laden and childlike.

Sometimes you find yourself repeating yourself for the hundredth time because there's nothing else you want to say. So I did it. 'I love you, Braslav.'

Almost to my disbelief I felt Braslav dissolve as I held him in my arms. My big strong older man, who together with the *chef de train* was managing an emergency that involved the lives or deaths of some sixty people, now lay in my arms and shook as he wept. He said what you already know he said, but I'll write it anyway.

'I love you too, Nedim,' was what Braslav said. And in the hour that followed he proved it.

NINE

Nedim…

I found Braslav beautiful naked. And he had a beautiful penis. It wasn't as big as mine, but its sheer elegance made up for that. Apart from anything else it was equipped with a slithery foreskin which mine, in the Muslim tradition, was obviously not. I could have spent the whole of the short night just playing with that: the first of its kind I'd ever handled, but Braslav had other ideas. He removed my hand from it and said, 'Don't. You'll make me come and it'll go to waste. I want to come inside you.'

I had never thought of myself as a submissive person. I'd fucked two women in the past, after all. But last night I had let Braslav try to penetrate me, just as I'd tried in my turn to penetrate him. I was more than willing to let him have first try again tonight. Not because he was a bit older than me, but because he was Braslav.

I lay on my back naked. My dick lay up the centre line of my belly, pointing towards my navel and – for the first time in my life, I saw to my astonishment – almost reaching it. I relaxed and waited to see what Braslav would do, wondering whether he would have more success than he'd had last night. I doubted it. Silently I wished him luck.

To my surprise Braslav reached down under the bunk

and picked something up. It was the small bottle of olive oil that had been part of our dinner's cruet set. I hadn't seen Braslav put it aside when Andrea collected the dishes but he obviously had. I had to be impressed by his forethought. Now he poured a little of the liquid onto his middle finger and inserted the finger into me. 'It's cold,' I couldn't help saying, and I saw my dick tremble with the sudden shock of it.

'Sorry,' said Braslav, 'but it'll soon warm up.' He was right. It soon did, and I found I was enjoying the sensation of his finger exploring the inside of me. Then he kind of fell forward on top of my chest and we kissed.

I couldn't see what happened next, but I felt it. Felt Braslav's finger pop out of me and felt him thrust his cock – he'd clearly also oiled that – inside me in the finger's place. I felt it go in like a piston into a cylinder. So easily it went. Why had we not thought of this source of lubrication last night? After all, we didn't leave our loco's cylinders un-oiled, un-greased. Never mind, I thought. At least tonight we were getting it right.

As Braslav slid slowly into me I felt a sensation like a lump rising inside my neck. It was as though his penis was also pushing into my throat. It felt strange at first, but soon I realised that I rather liked it. As for Braslav, he was clearly in ecstasy. I could feel it in his body, in the way he started to thrust into me with total abandon, I could see it in the expression on his face.

'Oh fuck, I'm going to come,' he said suddenly, and then he did, pumping himself into me with rapid piston strokes, and I could feel the slap-slap of his balls against my buttock cheeks.

It took him some time to pump himself all out but at last he was spent. Then he flopped on top of me and whispered, 'I love you, Nedim.' I liked that very much.

We lay together for twenty minutes or so, Braslav still inside me and at first still stiff. But at last I felt his organ deflate and then it slipped out unexpectedly with a little noise, which made us both laugh.

I discovered while Braslav was fucking me that I wanted to be inside him at the same time as he was inside me: wanted to be fucking him while he fucked me. This was anatomically impossible, I realised; it was a disappointment that I – and all men who like sex with other men – must learn to live with. Instead I said now, once Braslav's dick had fallen out of me, 'I want to do you now, Braslav.'

'Hmm,' he said, still lying on top of me. 'I think you may have to wait a bit.' Then he added, an apologetic note coming into his voice, 'Never done this before. I'm not very experienced. Didn't know what to expect.'

'I'm inexperienced too,' I said to reassure him. 'I've had two women, but never done anything with a man. Till just now.'

'You've still done more than me, though. I've only ever jacked men off in toilets. Never been with a woman. Never had a fuck.'

'Well, you've made up for that tonight,' I said.

'I came too soon,' he said.

'It doesn't matter,' I told him. 'We both enjoyed the experience. That's all that matters.' I thought for a second and a rather grand phrase came into my head. 'It's an aspect of love,' I said, and hoped that didn't sound too pompous.

It evidently didn't, for Braslav picked the sentence up. 'You're right,' he said. 'It's an aspect of love.'

I said, 'If I fucked you now, that would be another aspect, would it not?' That was a bit naughty of me; happily it made Braslav laugh.

'I'm still not sure about that,' he said. He reached under himself and gave my erection a tweak. 'You're very big. Head on yours like a piston. Like a plumber's suction cup.'

'Oil works wonders, I've heard,' I said. I giggled. I'd got into that sort of mood.

'All right, then,' I heard Braslav say. 'I'll let you try. But if it hurts you've got to stop. All right?'

'I promise,' I said.

Then Braslav climbed off me. 'Do it differently,' he said. 'Do me from behind, like a dog. I'll kneel beside the bed...'

So we both got off our bunk and knelt naked by the

bunk-side, the way I'd been told that Christian children said their prayers. Actually Braslav sprawled the top half of himself across the bunk and spread him arms out like someone about to be whipped. I knelt behind him, prising his knees apart with my own pair. I reached for the oil bottle and anointed my finger with it, then pushed it into Braslav. I liked the feel of the inside of him and wiggled my finger about. 'Not too cold, I hope?' I asked.

'I wasn't going to mention it,' said Braslav.

I found myself suddenly trembling on the brink of orgasm. I said, 'I'm nearly coming. Hope this won't hurt but I've got to get on with it.'

I didn't wait for Braslav's reply: there was no time left. I pushed my cock into his cleft and to my surprise it immediately found his anus and slipped easily into it.

It was just as well that it went in easily, as I only had time to give it three thrusts before I ejaculated. More explosively than I'd ever done before, I thought, even though I couldn't see the result.

We weren't in as comfortable a position as we'd been in when Braslav had fucked me, lying on top of me on the bunk. We didn't stay kneeling where we were for twenty minutes. After about a minute, while I was still hard, I pulled out.

Braslav gave a little yelp of pain.

'Sorry,' I said.

'That rim you've got on your dick-head,' Braslav said. 'It was fine going in. But coming out it's a menace.'

'I'll remember next time,' I said apologetically. 'I'll do what you did and let it go down before pulling it out.'

'We live and learn,' said Braslav, twisting round and getting up. He reached back with a hand and stroked his buttock cheeks. 'Ow, that's sore.'

'Sorry,' I said again. Then teasingly, 'Do you still love me?'

Braslav grinned. 'You bet I still do,' he said.

Braslav...

I slept with my arms round Nedim, cuddling him through the whole of the short night. It wasn't the most comfortable way to sleep but it was by far the best, and the best night I'd spent in my life. My second night with Nedim. I wanted it to be like this every night now. But not with any man. Only Nedim would do. Nedim, the man I loved, was now the only man I wanted to love.

Live every day as though it will be your last was a well known motto. Now I thought that *Live every night as though it will be your last* was an even better one. The sad fact was that this was almost certainly the last night I would be able to spend with Nedim. After we were rescued, as we surely would be in the morning, I couldn't see how or when or where the next opportunity to sleep with him would present itself. But by now nothing else would do for me. I wanted to spend every night with Nedim. I wanted to live with him. That had become, literally overnight, the over-riding ambition of my life.

I lived in a shabby apartment in a run-down block in Belgrade. I shared the apartment with three other railwaymen. But I counted my blessings. At least I had a room to myself, small though it was, and cramped as the apartment as a whole was. Nedim had told me he lived in a similar way. Well, maybe in the course of time someone would move out of my apartment and Nedim would be able to move into it. Or the other way round. But that might not happen for years. And even then we wouldn't be sharing a room. Not in an out-in-the-open kind of way. If we did do that -if we did anything more open than quietly visiting each other's bedrooms after everyone else had gone to sleep – we would not simply be talked about. As I had intimated to Nedim when answering in a general way his question about what happened to homosexual men, the likelihood was that we would be subject to all kinds of abuse that was more than verbal. We would run the risk of being killed, or at the very least beaten up.

As I lay, suddenly wakeful in the early dawn, protectively cradling Nedim who was still asleep, I was conscious of a vast gulf between the unbelievably wonderful present moment and the long-term future. Our future was a prospect in which it seemed that this brief taste of paradise would be impossible to repeat.

In the shorter term, though, and on a less exalted,

more earthly, level of experience, I found myself pleased that we had overcome our failure to ejaculate on our first night together. It seemed that our success in this department before we went to sleep had only too literally opened the floodgates. For we had woken up just two hours after first climaxing inside each other and promptly sucked each other off. And now as I pressed my dawn erection into the small of Nedim's back and, reaching round, clasped his, he too woke up. He turned towards me and we immediately masturbated each other to our third triumphant orgasm during the few short minutes that remained to us before we had to get up.

Nedim…

When in the cold early morning light Braslav and I looked at the stock of coal that remained in the tender I found myself fancying that someone must have been helping himself to it in the night, so depleted did it look. 'It'll barely last the morning,' I said despondently as I opened the dampers and the fire-hole door and made the firebox up.

'We'll be rescued by then,' said Braslav. But I was quickly getting to know him very well. I knew that this was mere whistling in the dark. He was taking his policy of not crossing bridges till he came to them to a bit of an extreme, I thought.

We hadn't spent many minutes in the cab before the *chef de train* arrived on the plank path across the snow outside and called up to us. With him were his deputy the *contrôleur*, and a man we hadn't yet met. He turned out to be the senior member of the Compagnie who shared our carriage with us. They wanted to know about the coal stocks, and Braslav invited them up to have a look.

Suddenly I found that I was taking part in a meeting at which the matters being discussed were so important that they might mean life or death. Big questions were raised, among which there was one unanswerable one: would we be rescued today, or tomorrow, or not? We could only guess, depending how optimistic or pessimistic we felt. The next question, though, required a decision of us. Should we use the last of the coal to keep the train heated for a few more hours, or let the engine fire go out and use the remaining coal for the kitchen range? If the latter, then there would be enough fuel to provide hot food and drink for two or three more days. The *contrôleur* reminded us there was only one day's stock of food remaining. Coffee and tea, though, would last longer than that…

Let the firebox go cold and we wouldn't be able to drive the train away when rescue came… The *chef de train* said it was inconceivable they would attempt a rescue without an engine big enough to pull the whole train away with it. Then Braslav spoke. As a Croatian in his home country, and as the member of staff who drove this part of the route more often than anybody else, he had the most detailed knowledge of our whereabouts. 'There's a village about three miles to the south,' he said. He pointed away across the white waste. 'In clear weather you can see it easily from the train. You can see smoke rising from its chimneys. Supposing a party of us set out across the snow. Perhaps we could buy food. Find a way to get a message to the outside world…'

'Surely we would all get frostbite,' said the *contrôleur*. I noticed the *we* in his sentence. He at once gained my respect for the way he had automatically counted himself into the dangerous mission that Braslav had suggested rather than, by using the word *you*, automatically ruling himself out of it.

Suddenly I heard my own voice speak. 'We'd take the precaution of wearing the thickest possible clothes, boots and gloves.' That was me, intervening in a discussion that included a board member of the Compagnie. I wouldn't previously have believed I could do that.

'You're all very brave,' said the *chef de train*. 'Believe me, I've no doubt of that…' But whatever he wanted to say, he didn't get the chance to get it out.

'If we walk we may get frostbite,' said Braslav, sounding and looking very serious. It was if he was suddenly confronting all his bridges at once. 'But to stay where we are, without rescue… that carries the risk of death.'

'Gentlemen,' said the member of the Compagnie board. 'I propose a compromise. I suggest we sit today out. We have food and warmth enough. Rescue should – it must – be on its way by now. But if we're proved wrong on that score – if we're still stuck here tomorrow morning, then we should put our driver's plan into immediate effect.'

'There is one problem with that,' said Braslav. He looked out and up at the sky. 'Today the weather holds. Those clouds aren't going to drop snow. By tomorrow morning we may be in the jaws of a blizzard again. Then my plan can't be carried out. We'll be stuck in an even more desperate situation than at present.'

'Then let me propose,' said the *chef de train*, 'a compromise between one compromise and another one.' He looked at his watch. 'Six o'clock. An hour till sunrise. I suggest we wait one more hour after that. If rescue hasn't come by then we put the driver's plan into practice. There'll still be some nine hours of daylight left. During the next two hours we can decide exactly who will be members of the scouting party. We can collect warm clothing from every available source. And meanwhile there are other jobs to do. Kitchen and waiting staff can carry the remaining coal through to the kitchen store, while our friends the driver and fireman...'

I think I guessed what was coming next. The wash-basin outlets had frozen, so it was futile to waste coal heating the water used for washing in the carriages. Also, there were far too many waste-pipes – one from each compartment – for all to have fires lit beneath them and be unblocked. On the other hand...

Braslav and I spent the next hour lighting fires beneath three of the train's toilets, unblocking the outlets from the wash-basins in those as well as the outlets from the pans themselves. But this time I was very careful where I positioned myself.

TEN

Nedim…

It was decided that Braslav would lead the scouting party. He spoke the local language and was himself a Croat. Then that I would go with him. This was something both Braslav and I insisted on. It was unthinkable that we wouldn't be together in this, and we were heedless of what others might deduce about the nature of our relationship from our combined insistence on setting out together on this adventure. Nevertheless we cloaked our determination not to be separated with the explanation that, although I was not from Croatia, I too spoke Serbo-Croat.

Two others would come with us. One was the restaurant-car chef. Though he was Swiss and spoke no Serbo-Croat, it was he who would have to prepare and cook whatever produce we might manage to find. Also, bearing in mind that we would be travelling across deep snow in an unforgiving environment, there was the fact that he was built like an ox.

The other member of our team was to be Andrea, to my private delight. I wondered if Sacha had had misgivings about letting his young man go, or if there had been a painful moment between them when they learned they would have to spend the rest of this frightening day apart. But it was no business of mine and so I was determined not to ask.

We put on two pairs of thick socks each, like mountain climbers, and boots a size bigger than the ones we normally took. We used the compartment that Braslav and I slept in as a changing room. Andrea was familiar with our compartment but I could see the chef looking around the place and clearly wondering a bit.

We had our knapsacks on our backs with, inside them, coffee in Thermos flasks, and brandy in a hip-flask. That was all. Braslav looked at his pocket watch as we stepped down from the corridor exit onto the snow beneath. It was exactly eight o'clock.

At first the going was easy. It was like the walks you do as a child, when snow has come down thick overnight. But walking on snow into which your legs sink almost to the knee at each step soon tires you. When you are a child and get tired of walking in the snow you can turn round and go back. That was not a possibility in our case.

Our world was white. The train diminished in size and importance behind us. It became a line of metal, half buried in the drifts. Soon it was out of sight. All around us the air was dull and silent. Where were the birds? The bare trees we passed from time to time were empty of leaves and empty of life. The sky was grey above and around us, enfolding us in light flurries of snow at times. Because there were always a few flurries between us and any point on the horizon the distance we could see was limited. It was like walking in a light white mist.

We didn't waste energy talking. Anyway, what would

we have talked about? Although the four of us walked only a yard or two apart we felt profoundly isolated from one another. We had nothing to do but think. At least, I was thinking. I presumed the others were doing likewise.

Braslav...

Normally I tried not to look too hard into the future, to imagine what life held in store for me. In fact I habitually did the opposite: I tried hard *not* to think about it. But now was different. This moment of walking through the endless cold and silent whiteness was making everything different. Already I had found myself imagining what the future might hold for Nedim and me. Since our first night in bed together I had found myself thinking of almost nothing else. Finding myself out here with nothing to do beyond putting one foot in front of the other intensified and clarified my thoughts.

One possibility was that we would die together in the snow. Either in the course of this risky adventure or else, if we were not rescued, back at the train. What would it be like when two people as much in love as Nedim and I were died at the same time? Would it be like walking through a doorway together, hand in hand? Finding ourselves still holding hands in a sun-warmed flower-filled garden on the other side of it? For there was no possibility that a different, separate Paradise awaited people of Nedim's faith and people of mine. As Sacha had said, all routes to truth led to the same place, just as all railway lines converged on Trieste.

All routes to truth, all routes to God, all routes to

Paradise. Suddenly I became despondent just seconds after this happy thought had entered my head. There was no Paradise for sinners such as Nedim and myself. The teachings of our two religions alike made outcasts of us.

Did we believe those teachings though? Probably neither of us did. If there was no God there was no everlasting fire of punishment, and that would be a relief. But then there was no heavenly doorway to walk through together. We couldn't have it both ways. If there was no God, no afterlife, then though we might die together Death would eternally separate us. That I thought was the worst of punishments. Eternal separation from the man I loved. Perhaps even eternal flames, shared together, would be better than that.

Better that we didn't die, though. At least not yet. Better that we made it through the snow and back to our train with plenteous food to eat. Better that we were rescued and taken to… Presumably Trieste. Where, as Sacha said, the routes of the world all met. There I would, I supposed, spend a night with Nedim in a railwaymen's hostel before taking the train back, exactly as we had been scheduled to do – except a few days late…

Then back to Belgrade. To our separate apartments, separate work schedules, separate lives. Or, might it happen, might it come to pass, that Nedim would be promoted to fireman permanently on the Orient Express? That we would be given the same shifts to work, sharing the footplate thrice weekly on the journey to Trieste, with a shared hostel room there that was ready to welcome us every two or three days? It was an idyllic picture of the future: Nedim and I working side by side all day every day and only having to spend one night in three apart. But I had to banish the thought. Railway rosters didn't work like that. While if we were to request such an unusual arrangement our bosses would quickly work out what was going on between us and we would be exposed and disgraced.

Perhaps we could run away together instead. To some country where people like Nedim and me were accepted as part of the social fabric, not ostracised or harassed but made to feel normal and safe. But was there such a place? I doubted that even America would answer to our need. And even if it did, or some other place did, then what would become of us, arriving penniless on a foreign shore, unable to speak the country's language...?

Arriving penniless. I was suddenly struck by a terrible thought. I wondered if I ought to mention it to the others. I decided not to. We would cross that bridge when we came to it.

Nedim...

We walked in a disorienting world of grey and white. There was no north nor south, no east nor west. Only by constantly looking back at our deep leg-prints could we be sure we were heading straight. Heading in the direction in which Braslav had said the village lay. And we had to take his word for that. Sometimes there is no other thing to be done than to trust another person. That can be a daunting, frightening thing to do. It was only marginally easier, I was discovering today, when you and the other person were in love.

Though what was love? Giving yourself. Surrendering yourself. Oh yes, and enjoying doing it.

We stopped occasionally to sip tea from our Thermos flasks. We seemed to make no progress, as I imagined it must be with ships out of sight of land that can only see the headway they've made by reference to the minute changes in the positions of the stars each night. In our world now the only things that were moving quickly were the hands of Braslav's watch.

We had set out at eight exactly. Somehow, in the excruciating cold and aching tiredness of our legs it became eleven o'clock. In those three hours had we made two miles? Or just one? Or had we missed the village and walked on past it? We had no means of knowing any of that. We could look back only on that line of dark footprints that vanished in the snowy mist.

Ahead of me there was a sudden shout. It came from Roman, the restaurant chef. He pointed ahead. There, coming and going in the misty flurries, was something in the air that was darker than the snow and clouds were. It rose almost directly ahead of us, only very slightly to the left of our course. It would hover in the air for a second or two, then be obliterated by the swirling mist. It was smoke.

We clasped hands, all four of us, then hugged each other, jumping up and down once or twice with exhilaration and joy. 'You were right,' said Roman to Braslav in a very man-to-man sort of way, while hugging him and clapping him on the back.

'And he took us in the right direction too,' I put in. I hugged Braslav then, and wanted desperately to kiss him and tell him of my admiration and love but I dared not.

Instead I asked, in a business-like way, 'How far do you think it is?'

'A mile?' suggested Braslav and the others nodded. Braslav's had been the triumph, he had earned his leadership. Nobody, for now at any rate, was going to contradict anything he said.

Braslav had said the village was about three miles south of where the train had ended up. If we had covered only two of them in three hours that meant it would take us a further exhausting hour and a half to cover the remaining distance. I buried that thought, that calculation, as we continued to walk towards the smoke. I guessed that we all buried it.

However, it was infinitely more cheerful, infinitely less frightening, to be heading for a destination we could see, however distant it might be, rather than towards one we couldn't. As we came closer to it the smoke divided itself. It was rising in several pillars from a place we couldn't yet see. It came, undoubtedly, from a human habitation. Chimney smoke. It rose straight up for some distance in air that was almost windless: that was a mercy for which we'd already privately given thanks.

Higher up the smoke wafted sideways then drifted down again as it chilled in the freezing air.

Gradually the dull grey, white-capped shapes of small buildings came into focus. Then we saw a scene that must have remained unchanged for centuries. Two rows of cottages that were little more than hovels faced each other across what in normal times must have been a roadway or lane but which was now a lake of slush, snow and manure in which a few pigs and chicken splashed about. Although footprints could now be seen heading off and back in all directions – presumably there were animals in nearby fields that needed tending – there were no people about. All the houses had their doors and window shutters firmly closed. Only the smoke rising energetically from the chimneys indicated that the cottages' occupants were at home, inside their doors, keeping warm as best they could.

The noise of sawing alerted us to the fact that at least one person was out and about. As we turned into the watery street we saw two men with a very old-style double-handled saw working on either side of a sawing-horse. A large pile of cut logs was on one side of them, an impressive stack of tree-branches on the other. Their breath steamed in great wreaths. They were doing exactly what we had been doing yesterday: cutting the fuel the population needed in order not to die of cold.

They saw us and almost jumped in surprise. Then one reached down and picked up a long-handled hammer from the ground beside him, while the other leaned down and picked up the two iron wedges that they'd been using to split the bigger logs with. He raised his hands level with his head and pointed the wedges towards us like two daggers, while the man with the hammer held it out in front of him. He swung it about a bit tentatively. Had he done more than that he'd have lost control of it: it was very big.

'We come in peace and friendship,' I heard Braslav call out. He sounded rather melodramatic, I thought, but the situation itself was a bit melodramatic. Had Braslav been rehearsing his words as we approached? I wondered. 'We are unarmed…'

'Not true,' yelled one of the two men, jabbing one of his iron wedges in the direction of Roman. Startled, I turned and looked at the chef. He had taken a pistol from inside his coat and was pointing it. No-one had discussed the carrying of weapons before we left. At least Braslav and I hadn't. All right, the Balkans were the Balkans, but we had reckoned without the gun-culture of the Swiss.

Braslav, also turning rapidly towards Roman now shouted, 'Put it away!' and, presumably because Braslav had won his spurs in getting us here and was therefore undisputed leader of our party, Roman did. Braslav turned to the two men. 'You can drop your hammer and wedges. You won't need them. We are fellow-Croats. We come from a train that is stuck in deep snow on the line towards Brod. We need to tell people where we are. Do you have working telegraph? We also need food.'

The two men lowered their hands, but didn't let go of the tools they held. 'Our telegraph hasn't worked for a week,' said the man with the wedges. 'We are in desperate straits. We have seen no police or agent of the state for the last fortnight, in this most desperate winter in living memory. We are nearly starving. Now you turn up and ask us to supply food!'

'It's desperate for you,' said Braslav, 'but it's also desperate for us.'

'How many are you on this train of yours?' said the peasant.

Braslav said, 'About forty,' I think. I was prepared to let him do the talking. It would have confused things if I'd jumped in, especially if Braslav was going to have to negotiate something difficult. The other two could not have intervened verbally even if they'd wanted to: neither spoke more than a word or two of Serbo-Croat. I alone could follow the conversation between Braslav and the peasant, though no doubt Roman and Andrea could catch the tone of it.

'Forty?!' said the peasant. Although by now we were standing close to him his exclamation was almost a shout. 'You come to a village of twenty persons who are nearly starved to death and ask for food for forty!'

The other man, the one with the hammer, had been silent up to this point. Now he spoke. Looking at us through narrowed eyes, and measuring his words like spoonfuls of some rare spice he asked Braslav, 'Exactly how much money have you brought?'

ELEVEN

Braslav…

Penniless. There would have been no point my bringing the matter up when it first went through my mind. Not unless we'd still been within sight of the train. But we'd been walking for an hour and a half at least, and there had been no going back by that stage. Now, however, was the moment for crossing this particular bridge. It would be a rehearsal, I thought in a sudden rush of black humour, for the moment when Nedim and I arrived in New York, broke.

I looked at the others. 'They need paying for any food they give us. How much have we got?'

Roman dipped into an inside pocket. I was relieved to see it wasn't the one with the pistol in it. 'The *contrôleur* gave me the *liquide*.' I knew that was the French word the Compagnie used for petty cash. I also knew they didn't keep much on board. The Orient Express was supplied on account at the various stations we stopped at where provisions were loaded. Most emergencies would be dealt with by the railway companies of the countries we went through, and presumably haggled over at a high level afterwards. So when Roman showed me what he had I was not surprised to see that it consisted of only a few bank-notes and coins in French francs, English pounds and American dollars.

I took a sample of each currency from him and

showed the notes and coins to the two peasants, trying to pretend that these items represented a substantial stock of cash. But the peasants were neither fooled nor impressed. They shook their heads and the one with the hammer snarled the word, 'Dinars,' the Yugoslavian currency.

Nedim and I looked at each other, shrugged our shoulders and dipped into our own pockets. We didn't have much between us, but we held it out. The time for pretending was past.

'For that we will give you two chickens, two loaves of bread and four eggs,' said the other peasant.

'In Belgrade,' began Nedim in a tone of outrage, 'we could buy…'

I stopped him with a hand on his arm. 'We are in no position to argue,' I said to him in German, hoping that the peasants might not understand that language. I turned to Roman and translated the peasants' offer for him. He shrugged, then nodded his head.

I turned back to the peasants. 'Please can you include some logs – and a shutter or something we can use as a sledge to take the things back. We will need more supplies tomorrow, you can see that is obvious. We will come back next time with gold.'

I felt Nedim's surprise in the air beside me. He was probably wondering where in the world we would get gold from. I know I was. The other two could only guess at what I might have just said.

Slowly the two peasants nodded to each other and then nodded at us. 'Come inside,' said one of them. 'We'll get the chickens first.'

I told the others what the man had said, asking if they were all right with the idea of going into a house that might be a trap. But they all nodded their heads. Roman and Nedim were big and muscular, while Andrea was, like me, wiry, strong and tough. The peasants were not that big, either. We reckoned we'd be all right.

The men dropped their makeshift weapons at that point and led us to the door of one of the shuttered cottages.

Inside, the darkness took some getting used to. A couple of candles twinkled in the gloom and a fire glowed red in the hearth but that was it. Meanwhile furred and feathered things we could barely make out with our eyes brushed against our legs. There was a sudden squawk. One of the peasants had grabbed a chicken from the floor and was wringing its neck. Meanwhile our eyes could now make out the form of an old woman sitting on the floor beside the hearth and stirring something in a pot.

'Make coffee,' our host instructed the woman, and in silence she got up to fetch another pot into which she poured water from a jug. The man who had wrung the chicken's neck now brusquely handed it, dead but still kicking, to Roman. With his hands free once more the peasant lunged after a second bird. The chickens were thoroughly panicked now and their squawks and feathers

107

filled the room as they scurried, wings flapping, round it. The second man meanwhile had taken four eggs from a box on a shelf and, opening a cupboard, searched in the darkness inside it for a couple of loaves of bread.

Coffee materialised after about five minutes. So did other peasants. They came in, opening the door without knocking, to see what was going on, alerted no doubt by our voices earlier and now by the chickens' squawking. After some explanations and discussion a box was brought from an outhouse and our provisions stowed within it. Someone even went off and came back with a disused door, to which someone else attached a length of rope.

The atmosphere improved minute by minute. Suspicion might not have been banished, but open hostility had been replaced by a sort of grudging interest in our story and predicament. Someone went out and then re-appeared with a bottle of fiery potato and fennel seed schnapps. I had never felt more in need of a drink.

Nedim...

Andrea had scarcely spoken during the long trek. I worried about his feelings, and wondered if he was frightened or overwhelmed by the experience. I felt guilty that I hadn't talked to him, but I needed it to be clear that it was Braslav I belonged to and cared most about. And in fact Braslav and I hadn't found much to say either. Then, when we were confronting the peasants, Andrea hadn't spoken at all. But neither had he flinched. He'd stood stock still while the hammer swung and the wedges were raised, and I admired him for that.

I admired Braslav even more, though, and I'd never admired or loved him more than at this moment. Now, with a glass of kummel in my hand and its contents beginning to warm my heart, I found I wanted to tell Andrea that. I put my arm around his shoulder and he rewarded me by turning and smiling his surprise into my face. Then it was my turn to be surprised, as Andrea spoke, and took my own words from my mouth.

'You are lucky to have Braslav for a man friend,' Andrea said. 'He may be small like I am, but he is handsome, clever and brave.'

'You're not small,' I blurted out. The kummel was making me incautious. It was less than forty-eight hours since I'd first tasted alcohol after all. 'You too are brave and beautiful. And your man Sacha is also very handsome and a wonderful man.'

We were speaking in German, of course, which Roman and Braslav perfectly understood. At once Braslav reprimanded me. 'Don't let the alcohol loosen your tongue too much.'

'I was only trying to praise you, Braslav,' I said, feeling the sting of tears under the lash of Braslav's gentle remark.

'It's all right, Braslav,' Roman said, touching him on the arm and trying to make the moment light. 'I'm aware of Sacha's sexual preference and of Andrea's too, though I don't share it. I've just this second learned about you and Nedim, and it took me a bit aback. But we're all friends here, in the middle of nowhere, when big things are at stake. We've risked our lives for each other today and so the normal conventions seem a bit unimportant. In any case I believe in Live and let live. That's the Swiss way. Your secrets, if they are secrets, will be safe with me when we get back.'

We had guessed the peasants had little knowledge of German, and their lack of interest in this conversation of ours proved us right. But it now became evident that they were not entirely ignorant of the language. One of them picked up on one word. *'Geheimnisse?* Secrets?' he asked suspiciously. 'What secrets?'

'It's all right,' Braslav said to him in Serbo-Croat, and in a placatory tone of voice. 'We were talking about our home lives in Belgrade and the private secrets of love.'

All the peasants chuckled at this, and the suspicious one's mind seemed to have been put at rest. The remark certainly thawed the atmosphere a little further. Meanwhile I felt even more proud of Braslav. I looked across at him lovingly. But to my surprise his eyes did not focus on me and they remained unsmiling, while his face was tense and his jawbone set.

Braslav...

I was talking to one of the peasants when, out of the corner of my eye, I saw Nedim put his arm around Andrea's shoulder. I tuned in to what Nedim was saying. He was calling Andrea brave and beautiful. I felt as though the ground had been cut away from under my feet. After all we had been through today… After all the efforts I had made to conquer my innate timidity, by leading a reconnaissance party in deep snow and cold – and I had made those efforts purely in order to impress Nedim, to court him and to look big in his eyes – here was Nedim telling Andrea that it was Andrea he admired. Andrea, who had done nothing all day but follow where I led … and look beautiful, I had to grant him that. Andrea also had the advantage of being about ten years younger than I was. Thus do all the efforts we make in pursuit of love go to waste…

Nedim…

We braced ourselves and set out again across the snow. We followed our footprints, which had been made less distinct but not yet filled by the light snow flurries. We took it in turns to drag the sledge. The box of food was pathetically light but we'd been given a generous supply of logs, and the logs filled the space available on the sledge and weighted it.

Braslav had talked little on our outward journey. On the return leg, though, I became aware that he was not just *not talking*. He was positively not wanting to talk. I could see it in the set of his jaw and shoulders as he strode ahead. I could read it in the way he moved his feet.

I caught him up. 'Braslav,' I said, 'What's the matter? Have I done something? Why don't you want to talk?

'Save your breath,' he answered me. 'We both need all our energy for walking. We want to get back alive, don't we? If you want to tell me something, then save it for when we get back.'

I could hardly believe what was happening. I had only known Braslav for two days. In that time I had fallen deeply in love with him. Deeply enough for me to realise I'd never known love before: never known anything like it. And I knew in the depths of whatever insight I was blessed with that the same went for Braslav too. We were now sharing the biggest and most mortally dangerous adventure of our lives. How could he behave like this?

I couldn't maintain my dignity then. Couldn't hide from the others the depth of what I felt. I burst into tears. Tears which I felt freezing as they ran down my face. I threw my arms around his shoulders. 'Braslav,' I cried, 'You're hurting me. Please don't do this.'

'Let go,' he answered roughly. 'Not here. Let it wait.' Roughly he shook me off. I was aghast, my world crushed and shattered like an egg in Braslav's fist.

'It can't wait,' I heard a voice say. But it was not my voice. Nor was it just one voice. Two voices spoke together. Andrea's and Roman's. One took hold of Braslav's left shoulder, the other took his right. Andrea and Roman spoke in a kind of chorus. One after the other. I no longer remember which of them said what.

'You misheard,' one of them said. The other, 'You

misunderstood.' And then, 'The cold is getting to you.'

'Don't patronise me,' Braslav shouted and tried to shake them off. With Andrea he succeeded. Andrea went sprawling across the snow and fell into it raising a cloud of crystals and mist. But Roman was too big for Braslav to shake off, and he clung to him.

'Your young man loves you,' Roman said to Braslav. 'I heard him, while you were talking Serbo-Croat. He was telling Andrea how much you meant to him. He added that Andrea looked nice – which he does, as even I will admit – as a simple compliment. He was being polite. You must understand that. You have a future with Nedim. The cold may be playing tricks with your brain, but you must understand that.'

'I'll think about it,' Braslav said ungraciously. 'Plenty of time to think as we walk.' But then he went over to where Andrea was picking himself up. He helped him to his feet, both of them floundering in the deep snow. 'I'm sorry,' he said to Andrea, and I heard his voice choke as he said it.

'It's all right,' Andrea said with frosty dignity as he dusted himself off. And then the four of us set off again in the snow, most literally retracing our morning's footsteps. We walked in almost total silence for three hours, and it was the longest and most awful walk of my life.

Braslav...

I didn't know how we would get back. We had eaten

nothing since early morning, and, except for those few minutes inside a peasant hovel drinking coffee and schnapps, had been out of doors, struggling in deep snow for hours. I could feel my heart pumping like a steam engine on a steep climb with the strain of all of it. But bigger and worse than all of that was something else: I carried a weight inside me that was bigger than the sledge we took turns to pull. It was bigger than the responsibility I seemed to have shouldered in trying to get the four of us back to the train alive and intact. It was the weight of not knowing whether the others had spoken the truth or not. Perhaps it was true, what they had said. That I'd missed a sentence or two in what Nedim had said. That he loved me no less for the fact that he clearly found Andrea attractive.

Perhaps that was all true. Nevertheless, small things – if this was a small thing – tell us big things. The big thing was that Nedim was younger and more desirable than I was. Other men, perhaps younger than he was, would inevitably catch his eye. If even a few more weeks were granted to us by whatever power existed Nedim would inevitably be swept off his feet by someone else. If his head could be turned so easily by someone with as little to offer as I had, then I would have no chance when someone else came along who was younger and more attractive... I tried to concentrate on putting one foot in front of the other as we walked through the afternoon's dwindling light. Perhaps Nedim would have something to say to me when we returned to the train. To our cosy compartment. To our bed...

Nedim…

I saw the tears flowing, freezing, down Braslav's face as he walked alongside me, determined to set us a good example as he placed one foot ahead of the other, and as we all took turns to pull the sledge that got heavier and heavier as the hours passed. I knew I could do no good by trying to say more while we continued on our journey through the cold vastness. So I bit my tongue. I would have to wait till we were back in the privacy of our bedroom compartment before we could begin to sort this out. The afternoon wore thin and grey as the chilled hours fled to meet the oncoming night. Soon it would be dark, and there was no sign yet of the train ahead of us; only our leg-prints of this morning stretched mockingly ahead of us.

The sledge continued to grow heavier and heavier. But its heaviness came nowhere near to the heaviness that, as I began to contemplate a future without the love of Braslav to sustain and feed and warm me, grew in my heart.

TWELVE

Braslav...

Andrea saw it first. Shouted and pointed at it. A dark line against the greying whiteness in the dusk. As we got closer we could see that the windows were lit. A great wave of feeling swelled up inside me at the sight. Extraordinarily, thoughts of my dead mother came into my heart and I imagined her as she was when I was very young, at the lit open door of the train, welcoming us home. I'd already been crying a lot, because of my feelings about Nedim, so the extra burst of tears this vision caused me hardly noticed. But then, looking round at the others, I saw all three of their faces also streaked with tears. Of course it might just have been the cold.

Nedim...

I haven't words to express the emotional nature of that return to the train. It was like the biggest homecoming of my life. One or two passengers spotted us through the windows, then they must have told the others for soon the windows were black with the heads of people looking out. Once or twice someone opened a window in the freezing cold and shouted hurrahs of encouragement to us.

At last a figure came ploughing towards us through the tracks we'd made as we set out. Wearing only ordinary shoes and coat. It was Sacha. When he reached us he grabbed hold of his Andrea and they held each other tightly and as though they could never bear to let go, beyond caring what Roman or the watching passengers might think. They had no words for each other yet, exchanging only their urgent caresses. There was no doubt in my mind now that the two of them were as much in love with each other as Braslav and I were, and that their enforced parting earlier today had been a wounding experience for them both.

Braslav...

My heart gave me no choice. When, after watching the joyful reunion of Sacha and Andrea, Nedim felt compelled to embrace me, I could not repel him again, but held him to me, feeling his heart pounding against the pounding of my own. I'd heard the expression, *Two hearts that beat as one,* but fully understood it only now, at this most intense moment of my life.

Then I saw that there was no-one to greet and embrace Roman. I took my head away from Nedim's neck for a second and saw Roman, standing huge and alone beside us in the snow, with tears of relief coursing silently down his face. 'Come here,' I said to him, and he did, and for a moment or two Nedim and I enveloped him in a shared embrace.

At last we all detached ourselves and walked the final hundred yards to the snowbound train that had transformed itself into a precious home during our nine hours' absence. The *contrôleur* and the *chef de train* came out into the snow, followed by other colleagues of

Sacha and Andrea, and even some of the passengers, who were relieved and excited to see us, and clapped us on the back or hugged us. It was a true homecoming.

'Has the engine fire gone out?' I asked.

'I think so,' replied the *chef de train*. All is cold now, except the kitchen range.'

'We've brought logs, as you can see,' I said. 'Maybe we could make a fire in the firebox just big enough to stop the water freezing in the boiler and splitting the pipes. If we're not too late for that.'

'Do that,' said the *chef de train*. 'Then eat. Then get some rest.'

Meawhile Roman was showing the contents of the box. Two chickens, two loaves and four eggs, and forty people to eat them. I thought of the miracle of the loaves and fishes and wondered how we would manage without the intervention of Jesus Christ.

Nedim...

Poor 72619. How silent, cold and desolate she was. We dragged the sledge towards her, climbed into the cab, on the floor of which new snow now lay. I opened up the fire-hole door and poked around in the dead ashes with a rake. A little warmth came out at us, and that was something. I opened the dampers up. After a few moments I saw some sparks of red among the cinders, and called to Braslav, 'She's still alight.'

Braslav was checking the bleed-cocks on the pipe-work that ran through the cab. 'Water isn't frozen yet. We may be just all right.'

Braslav jumped down and handed up to me some of the logs that were piled on the sledge. I placed them carefully among the warm ash with a shovel, and hoped for the best.

We climbed up onto the tender tank and dipped it with a pole. The pole broke through a skin of ice, but the skin wasn't very thick. That was because the steam-pipe that fed heat to the train behind us ran through the water in the tender. It was designed that way precisely in order to stop the water freezing in winter. Today, despite the steam having died to nothing in the last few hours, the system had proved its worth.

While we were up on the tender top the door into our carriage opened and there stood Sacha looking up at us. 'You've worked enough,' he said. 'For God's sake come in and get warm and take your boots off. You've probably got frostbite. Andrea has.' That meant that Sacha had taken Andrea's boots off. The thought of that brought a lump to my throat. But lumps were coming very readily to my throat these last few days, I'd noticed.

'Follow Sacha,' I told Braslav. It gave me a feeling of excitement to be giving him a direct order for the first time. 'I'm just going to check the firebox, then I'll join you in half a minute.'

I was overwhelmed by my own feelings as I saw

Braslav meekly follow my instruction and climb down the back of the tender and follow Sacha inside our carriage. I, however, climbed down into the empty coal space, up the other side and down into the cab. The logs were alight and burning well, to my relief. I damped the fire and shut it up. It wouldn't heat the train, let alone create a head of steam, but at least the boiler and tender tank might not freeze during the night. If my calculations were wrong, and the pipes froze and the boiler blew to shrapnel in the night, well, we had done our best. The tender would stand between any flying metal and the place where Braslav and I would be lying in bed. I marvelled at my own equanimity. I had never before felt calm when confronting the possibility of a locomotive's boiler blowing up. But I knew why this was. It was entirely due to Braslav.

A minute later I was in the carriage and opening the door to our compartment. There stood Braslav, confronting me with a woeful face. 'I wanted to welcome you into a warm home of a place,' he said. 'Instead it's cold in here.'

Tears sprang to my eyes. If that was all he was worried about... 'It isn't fucking cold,' I said in a rasp of a voice. 'It's warm because you're here,' I said. I wrapped my arms around him. 'It's warm because we're us. Now sit down and I'll take your boots off.'

'I was thinking about the home I had as a child,' Braslav said; his voice was all choked up. 'How warm it used to be. Me and my mother...' He broke apart and cried at that point and I did too. Together we fell, locked in each other's embrace, onto our bunk. 'I wanted to make a home for you,' Braslav said in a wraith of a voice. 'I still want to do that.'

'You can,' I said. 'I want that too.' I wanted that more than I'd ever wanted anything on earth.

'I can't,' Braslav whispered. It was the best, right then, that he could manage with his voice. 'We can't. Everything's stacked against us. Our two religions. The society we live in. And then you won't be constant. Why should you be?'

'Me not be constant? What in the world are you talking about?' I was truly amazed by what Braslav had just said. His words punctured my rib-cage like a knife.

'You're young. You'll fly the coop. Young men do that. Even I know this. Two days we've known each other – just two days – and been in love about the same length of time. But already I hear you telling Andrea he's beautiful... What will it be like after two months, two years, or twenty?'

Now I understood. 'Braslav, don't be a fool,' I said. My voice too was just a husk. 'You didn't hear the conversation. Andrea and I were both praising you. We were both in awe of your leadership, your bravery, your handsomeness and your intelligence, we said. Then I thought that Sacha was not there to give words of praise to Andrea and that Andrea needed them at that moment. I said that he too was beautiful. It was no more than the truth. You're aware of Andrea's beauty as much as I am.

That doesn't mean we want to be unfaithful to each other with him.'

'You stood with your arms around each other…'

'Heavens!' I said. 'Not long ago we stood with our arms around Roman and Sacha and some of the passengers. We've been to hell and back, the situation has been dangerous and emotional. Emotional because it was dangerous. It's what soldiers do and feel in wartime. I'm not going to lose my heart to Andrea. The idea of that… When I'm more in love with you than I could ever be with anyone…' I couldn't speak any more. Neither could Braslav, I realised. But the way his arms, already holding me, tightened around me, and moved against my back, told me more eloquently than any words could have done, that he had understood what I'd said. Told me our moment – our four-hour moment – of misunderstanding was past. Told me how much he loved me, wanted me and needed me. Ah, the eloquence of a hug!

We would find a home together. Whatever it cost. However long it took. I decided at that moment that I would make the pursuit of that goal the main ambition of my life. I stroked Braslav's hair and he stroked mine. Then at last I said, 'Let's get you up now. Got to get those boots off…'

Braslav…

I had never before imagined that the removing of another man's boots could be an expression of the deepest and tenderest love, let alone that it could form the climactic healing moment in the making-up process that follows a lovers' tiff.

Though it wasn't really a tiff, was it? Just a misunderstanding on my part. Poor Nedim. Quite accidentally we had hurt each other deeply on the most testing day we'd undergone in our lives to date.

Nedim...

Poor Braslav.

Braslav...

We both had the first symptom of frostbite. The little toes of both our pairs of feet were numb and white. We rubbed each other's in our hands and tried to warm them up, though without much success. 'Our room's too cold,' I said again. 'It doesn't help.'

'It isn't cold,' Nedim protested. 'It's warm because of us.' He could be quite feminine at times, I realised: he could say things that were poetic and heart-warming without being of much practical use.

'Is your mother still alive?' I asked Nedim as he sat at my feet, like Jesus washing the apostles' feet.

'No,' he answered, 'she's dead.'

'Mine too,' I said. I knew we would talk much about our mothers in the times to come, if we were granted them, and that they would be big conversations and deep. 'Your father?' I went on.

'He appeared in my mother's life just before I was born... Well, nine months before, to be precise. Then disappeared a year or two afterwards. Came back again from time to time after that. I haven't seen him since I was eight. My mother died when I was twenty...'

I reached down and prised one of his hands away from my feet in order to hold it for a moment. 'My poor Nedim,' I said.

And yet his story wasn't so different from mine. A father who came and went. Who disappeared for good when I was twelve. My mother had died when I was twenty-eight. I told Nedim this.

'Were you an only child?' he asked me quietly.

'Yes,' I said.

'Don't quite know how,' he said, 'but somehow I'd guessed that.'

Nedim...

Somehow that was the most intimate moment we'd shared yet. Rubbing each other's toes and feet was hardly the most romantic of things to do and yet, weirdly, it was.

There came a knock on the door. I answered without getting up. Sacha entered. 'There will be food in another hour,' he said. 'In the restaurant car. Staff and passengers all together. For the sake of warmth. No distinctions now of class or role or status. We're all victims of an emergency. All in the same boat. On the other hand, the meal will not be very big.'

'We know that,' said Braslav with a wry laugh. 'We delivered it.' Then, very seriously he added, 'And tomorrow we are going back again. Proper provisions next time. But we need money…'

'Andrea has explained all that,' Sacha said. 'The villagers demanded gold. They shall have it. The *chef de train* has explained this to a meeting of the passengers. They have dug deep into their pockets.'

Since I had met Braslav my world had changed utterly. I'd been battered by experience after experience. (Quite apart from falling in love.) I'd been on the Orient Express. I'd survived a train crash. I'd tasted alcohol and was getting a taste for it. I was sleeping in the most opulently furnished bedroom I could have imagined. I'd slaved in the freezing cold, breaking coal for hours at a stretch, working like a convict. I'd been on a life or death adventure through the snow, pulling a sledge, like Scott or Amundsen in the Antarctic. Now, at dinner time on this third day came the strangest yet.

I was dining in the restaurant car among the passengers aboard the train, seated at a table with Braslav and Sacha and two other conductors. At nearby tables sat passengers, wrapped up now, quite unfashionably, in their scarves and overcoats. Among them, I recollected, was a doctor, an internationally famous detective and – perhaps, or almost certainly – a murderer who had got off scot-free… As they were all wrapped up like mummies I couldn't guess which was which. My mind went on boggling at all of this.

Our table was laid with cutlery of solid silver. The bone-china plates off which we ate were gold embossed. The meal was small – we knew it would be. Roman had eked out the chickens with left-over vegetables, and flavoured the gravy with paprika to give the too-fresh birds some oomph. The plates were garnished with the most minute slice of hard-boiled egg, and a nearly transparent slice of bread. Twenty slices from each loaf, by my calculation, ten from each egg. We were served by Andrea, who presently brought his own plate of food to our table and we all squeezed round to give him space. The restaurant car was more than packed. It hadn't been designed to take a whole trainload of passengers at once, let alone the large complement of staff. I asked Andrea, 'Will Roman join us?'

'When all the food is served,' Andrea said.

Braslav asked Andrea, urgent suddenly, 'Has he taken his boots off?'

'Not yet,' said Andrea. 'He hasn't had a moment…'

'He must take them off. He'll have frostbite starting. He needs to get them off and someone rub his feet before it takes hold and gets worse.' And with that Braslav got up from the table. Letting his damask napkin drop to the floor unheeded he threaded his way between the crammed tables and disappeared into the kitchen. I knew what he was going to do. I loved him all the more for it.

THIRTEEN

Nedim...

Only when everybody else had been served did Roman emerge from the kitchen. He joined our already overcrowded table, and a cheer went up from among the passengers as he did so, now back in his normal shoes and socks. It was ironical, I thought, that this Cordon Bleu chef, who usually went unacknowledged among the passengers despite creating dish upon magic dish night after night, should now be cheered to the roof after producing the poorest, smallest, most peasantly meal ever served in the forty-five year history of the Orient Express.

Yes, Roman too was suffering from the numbness of the little toes that the other members of our scouting party were experiencing. The doctor came away from the party he was sitting with and, standing by our table, first paid tribute to our courage and stamina, and then said that he would be happy to give us all a quick physical examination after the meal – in particular of our fingers and toes – to check that all was well.

Because the meal was so meagre the staff were more than generous with the wine. Perhaps in part because they were sharing it – I mean we were sharing it – with the passengers. Before it too ran out like the food. The wine loosened all our tongues, and the conductors who sat at our table began to exchange stories about the

Orient Express. About the time the train had run through the buffers at Frankfurt and broken through the wall into the station restaurant to the terror of all the people dining there. About the Armistice of 1918 being signed in one of the express's carriages. About the kings and princes and princesses who had travelled on the express. About the spies who met on it – the conductors were discreet employees of the Compagnie: for all the wine they were putting away they managed to name no names when talking of the spies – and about the many high-society romances, flirtations and improper liaisons and assignations that had occurred on board. When the discussion turned along this avenue Braslav and I exchanged significant smiles and raised-eyebrow glances more than once.

The story I enjoyed most was one concerning the introduction of Second- and Third-Class carriages just a dozen years before. There was a part of the train's route – well south of Yugoslavia, in Salonika – that ran alongside a broad river where, in summer, the local girls liked to bathe in the nude. Orders were given that the conductors should pull down the blinds on the windows of the Second- and Third-Class carriages as the trains approached this scene of temptation towards sinful thoughts. However the windows of the First-Class carriages remained un-curtained... Our whole table erupted into laughter when that story was trotted out.

We had fine wines from a region of France I had never heard of called the Médoc, and some from a nearby region called Cahors. It had been the favourite wine of the Russian Tsars. But since their disappearance ten years earlier there was no market for it. The Tsars had travelled often by the Orient Express, and so the Compagnie carried a big stock of Cahors wine, some of it going back years. It tasted extremely good, and we toasted the late Tsar gratefully. One man's downfall is another man's gain.

If the wine was going to the others' heads, then it was naturally going to mine – unused to it before two nights ago – even more. I got up at one point and treated my companions to a rendition of a simple Bosnian peasants' song. That set the ball rolling, and other members of staff as well as passengers began to get up and give us songs from their native lands. They included French, German and Italian songs. Turkish, Serbian, Greek and even American. Only the English seemed unwilling to join in. Perhaps the English couldn't sing.

I had a sudden inspiration. If Braslav and I could have the luxury of a sleeping compartment for the night – this night must surely be our last – then why should the same dispensation not be allowed to Sacha and Andrea? There was an empty compartment next to ours. I put this to Sacha.

'What a tempting thought,' he said, but he shook his head as he spoke. 'Unfortunately it cannot become a reality. My duty is to stay in the corridor all night on my divan, in case the passengers need anything in the night. For Andrea there would be no problem, as he sleeps in a hammock,' – he pointed around him – 'right here in the restaurant car.'

'And Roman?' I asked.

'He too has a hammock stretched across the restaurant car.'

I realised then that alcohol can wonderfully clarify one's thoughts and engender easy solutions to problems when no solution seemed possible before. I said to Sacha, 'What can passengers possibly ask for in the night now? There are no newspapers; no food is left… A bottle of mineral water maybe. Nothing more. Roman would know where supplies are kept…' I turned and spoke to Roman.

'Would you consider,' I said to Roman, 'spending this night on the divan in the corridor of Sacha's coach, taking the risk that you might be woken and asked for a bottle of water or two, in order to allow Sacha and Andrea one night of privacy in an empty compartment in the Athens-Paris coach?'

Roman looked startled for a moment by my question but then he answered it. 'I think that if my wife came on board tonight and someone else made such a generous offer, enabling the two of us to sleep the night together, I would gratefully accept. Therefore I shall propose that very thing to Sacha and his young friend.' He leaned around my back and spoke to Sacha in those terms. I heard the offer made most kindly, and the joyful surprise in Sacha's voice as he answered and accepted it. I gave thanks then for the benefits of alcohol and regretted those years that had gone before during which I had never tasted it.

Braslav...

After we had eaten, the doctor took the four of us who had been on the day's expedition into his compartment one at a time and did a few checks. He looked into our eyes, took pulses and temperatures and examined our hands and feet. I told him about the numbness in my toes. 'It's an early sign of frostbite,' he said. 'It may last for some time. Maybe even months. But your circulation has returned well. You've probably escaped anything worse. Whoever goes back out there tomorrow should take extra precautions, I suggest.'

'Such as?' I asked.

He smiled at me rather mischievously. 'Snowshoes might be a start,' he said.

The four of us compared notes afterwards. It seemed that all of us had escaped anything more serious than numb toes in the way of frostbite. Then, while the kitchen lads, having finished the washing-up, began to hoist their hammocks in the restaurant car, we made our way to bed, parting in the corridor where Roman would be bedding down in Sacha's accustomed place. I showed Andrea the empty compartment next to the one I shared with Nedim, and he went inside it to await Sacha there. I thought – like a bridegroom on his wedding night.

Nedim behaved extraordinarily once we had shut our compartment door upon us. He was all over me with kisses, eager as a puppy that hasn't seen you for ages. I had no objection to that of course. He then ripped my trousers down and started to suck me without attempting to undress either of us properly or to wait till we were tucked up in bed.

In bed it would be tonight; there would be no frolicking naked alongside it or on top of the blankets as on the previous two nights. The compartment was really cold now, and damp. If the log fire did its work it might just about send enough steam through the pipes to stop them freezing up, but it wouldn't heat the compartment. 'Come on,' I said. 'There'll be time for all that when we get into bed.'

I had to pull myself out of his mouth – an action he resisted strongly at first, and I became worried that he might bite my pulsing dick by accident. It wasn't that he had become unmanageably drunk, simply that the alcohol combining with his excitement had made him a bit reckless and heedless of consequences.

Eventually I undressed myself, while he collapsed onto the bed before I could stop him. Then I had to take all his clothes off him while he lay there – as if I were a hospital nurse. But that was the easy part. Trying to get someone who was bigger than I was underneath the bedclothes he was lying on top of without tipping him onto the floor proved a much more difficult task. He lay there looking lovely and showing off his hard prick while laughing bawdily… The alcohol seemed only now to be achieving its full effect. He could only manage to get one word out now, and he repeated and repeated it. 'Cold, cold, cold,' he said again and again.

'You will be cold if you don't help me get you under the sheet,' I said. 'And spare a thought for me. I can't get into bed until you do. I'm as naked as you are and I'm freezing my balls off.' Though I couldn't help laughing as I said it.

At last I managed to roll him to one side of the narrow bunk, then roll the free half of the blankets and top sheet up against him like a roll of carpet, and push him over the top of it. Then at last I could cover him up and join him inside the bed with chattering teeth and much relief. However by now he was already asleep.

And that was the story of the third occasion we went to bed in the same bunk.

Nedim...

I knew that non-Muslims suffered from a thing called a hangover the day that followed too large an intake of alcohol. I had never experienced such a thing myself. I had never guessed before the dawn of this new day how awful an experience it was.

I woke up with a head and limbs that ached as if I'd been kicked multiple times by a horse. I was so desperate for water that I could hardly manage to utter the words required to tell Braslav that I needed it. And when he, so full of concern and love for me in my pitiable state that my heart broke, went out into the corridor and returned with a bottle full of it, and I put it to my gasping mouth, the headache throbbed so much I thought my skull would break.

'If you don't want to come with us today…' Braslav began in a tender voice.

I interrupted him. 'I'm coming with you if it kills me. I wouldn't let you go without me even if I was dying. I'd only not come with you if I was already dead.'

I was angry with myself as well. I had just passed my third night with Braslav – which might well be my last night with him – without being conscious enough to enjoy the experience. I had wasted something immeasurably precious, and ruined the night for the man I loved. 'Oh fuck it, I'm sorry,' I said and tears welled up and ran, first warm but quickly cooling, across my cheeks.

'Don't be sorry,' said Braslav. He smiled a bit ruefully and stroked my hair as he said it. 'Welcome to the world of those of us who drink. What happened to you has happened to all of us. We learn, little by little, how to handle it.'

A moment later there was a knock at the door and Andrea came in with cups of steaming black coffee. He giggled at the sight of me, and the state of me, lying swaddled in blankets in the bunk. 'I'm afraid there's no brandy in the coffee today,' he said. 'Somebody stole one of the last two bottles during the night. Roman has hidden the final bottle, to be kept for emergency medical use only.'

'I don't think Nedim is going to mind there being no brandy this morning,' Braslav said.

Braslav...

This was the morning I found myself admiring Nedim for his tenacity and fortitude as well as for everything else. He got up and dressed himself without a word of complaint. Not even a groan escaped his lips. He led the way around the side of the tender and opened the fire-hole door before I could do it for him. Then, again without waiting for me to help him, he started piling the remaining logs into the firebox.

The *chef de train* arrived while we were doing this (I quickly did join in with the task, of course) and asked if we were still agreeable to setting out again on a second foraging expedition. He would completely understand if we wanted to relinquish the task to others...

Nedim, who had been almost silent since we had left our compartment, now found his tongue. He said that we two would most definitely be going. That we two alone spoke Serbo-Croat fluently and that the peasants now knew us. Also that it was with some considerable effort that we had won their trust. A new team would have to start from scratch. Of course the other members of the team didn't have to be Roman and Andrea...

'Roman and Andrea are as determined as you are,' the *chef de train* said. 'And there will be an additional member of the team. Sacha is also determined to join the expedition. For reasons which I am not supposed to know about but which ... um ... are becoming clearer as time passes.'

Something that was also happening as time passed was that the *chef de train*, who had earlier used surnames only when speaking about his staff, now used their first names freely. Thus do hard times make brothers of all of us.

'I have some things for you,' the *chef de train* continued. Until now he had been standing in the snow below the cab. Now he took hold of the vertical handrail and climbed the steps. Inside the cab he took a bag from his pocket and handed it to me. 'This is the gold we talked about. Inside your compartment meanwhile are thin boards to be tied on to the soles of your boots. Snowshoes, the doctor ordered, and the boys have done the best they could, adapting the sides of empty boxes of fruit.'

He then inspected the log fire and asked how long it would last. We could only guess. We said there was a good chance the pipes and boiler would not be frozen before we got back. He said we would find the other members of our party ready and waiting for us when we returned to our coach. There would be coffee, though it would be without milk. That, as well as the brandy, had run out. (He didn't know we knew about the theft in the night and that Roman had hidden the last bottle, and we didn't tell him that we did.) No food, however. There was nothing at all left after last night. In this, though, we would be in the same boat as everybody else, passengers and staff alike.

And so, equipped with snowshoes, armed with gold and coffee and Roman's gun, a little frightened, just like yesterday, about what might befall us, yet grimly hopeful, we set out. I, though, was armed and equipped with something else. Two other things, to be precise. My love for Nedim. And Nedim's love.

FOURTEEN

Nedim…

The snowshoes made an immense difference. Instead of plunging nearly knee-deep at each step, our feet sank only a few inches. We expended only a fraction of yesterday's energy, and moved at nearly twice yesterday's pace. We had the further advantages of knowing that we had made the journey safely once and could therefore do it again, and of having our own footprints to follow. They, and the sledge tracks, were a little indistinct in places as a result of wind-blown snow, but enough of them were visible to give us the guidance we needed.

Another reason for us to feel more confident, less anxious than yesterday, was an improvement in the weather. Snow was no longer falling from the sky, even in occasional flurries. Instead the clouds were lightening and thinning out. As the morning went on blue shapes began to sail among them and we were assured for the first time in many days that the sky was still blue above.

The drawback for me was the obvious one: I was suffering from my first ever hangover. So although so many things were making the going easier today, for me the going was still just as difficult. Last night I had come to the mistaken conclusion that alcohol was the magic bullet that made everything simple, all problems solvable, in life. This morning I felt ashamed of even flirting with such a thought. This morning alcohol was indeed a bullet. It felt like a cannon-ball lodged in the centre of my head. What kept me going, putting one foot in front of the other, was the healing knowledge that I was doing this for causes that were bigger than myself. The desperate need of all the passengers for food and warmth. That for a start. Then for the sake of Braslav. I wanted to redeem myself. I wanted to build myself up in his eyes after that. I wanted his approval, even if I could never deserve his admiration. I had a desperate need for his warmth.

Good things began to happen, though. In less than an hour and a quarter we caught sight of the village's rising smoke. By now more than half of the sky had turned blue overhead. And I made yet one more discovery about alcohol. Or about hangovers at least. If you can bear to take punishingly hard exercise while in the throes of one the exercise will eventually cure you of your pain – once you have gone through the barrier that the pain creates, smashed your way through the wall of pain itself.

Before we reached the village I felt light-hearted enough to ask Braslav, walking alongside him, at that moment out in front, 'When I was drunk last night, why didn't you leave me in the lower bunk with an extra blanket thrown on top of me? You could have made yourself comfortable on your own in the top bunk.'

Braslav gave me a quizzical look. 'Surely you know the answer to that,' he said. 'Would you have done that if our roles had been reversed?'

'Of course not,' I said indignantly. 'How could you imagine that?'

Braslav laughed loudly for the first time this morning. 'Then how could *you* imagine that? I've answered you, I think. Besides,' and then his voice and face became serious, 'you talked lightly of my being comfortable on my own. I shall never be comfortable on my own. I shall never be comfortable anywhere without you, Nedim. Not now that I've met you. Can you understand that?'

Braslav sometimes had a way of saying exactly what I knew in my heart but had not got into my head yet. 'Yes,' I said. 'Of course I understand. It's the same for me. It couldn't be more the same.'

Braslav...

I was the leader of the party, and in that role you are expected not to do anything that looks soft, such as publicly kiss the person you love. It's considered bad enough form if that person's a woman. But if they are male... As far as I knew there were no precedents.

I hesitated for a moment, then felt ashamed of even that second's doubt. The more so because two of the people trudging behind us were another male couple who loved, while the other, Roman, knew about us – and was highly sympathetic, it now appeared, in the light of his chivalrous agreement to sleep in the corridor last night so that Sacha and Andrea could share a compartment for one night.

I stopped walking, turned to Nedim and embraced

him, then covered his frozen lips with kisses, while holding the sides of his cold head. After the words he had just spoken to me I could do no less. I might still have done it had the whole trainload of passengers been following us. Still, the moment had necessarily to be brief. It had brought the other three to a respectful halt a few yards behind us. I couldn't hold them up for long. After all, I was the leader of the group and conscious of the responsibilities that went with that.

Nedim...

It seemed barely another half-hour before we found our way into the slush-filled main street of the village, dragging our empty sledge. (So important had that sledge become to us that we no longer saw it for what it had been till as recently as yesterday: a disused door from an outhouse.) Amazingly the sun came out as we arrived between the two rows of houses and although there was little warmth in that sun the chill was a lot less ferocious than yesterday's.

There were two or three children playing outside amidst the slush, but they ran back to their houses when they saw us. However the doors soon opened again and their fathers, some of the men we had met and drunk with yesterday, came out to greet us. Soon a small crowd had gathered around us. Braslav spoke. 'Today we have come better prepared,' he said rather seriously. 'We have brought gold with us.'

'How much?' asked one of the surlier peasants. He was the one who had swung the hammer at us.

'Enough to buy food for forty people for two days,' said Braslav, 'as well as a further supply of logs. What can you let us have?'

It took a little time but at last a deal was struck. We would be departing with two sheep and two goats – they were fetched from an outhouse and their throats were slit in front of us: they bled out onto the snow, crimsoning it. We were also given a sack that was half-filled with potatoes and then had cabbages thrown in on top. A second old door was found and brought to us and that was piled up with logs.

There was some haggling over the cost of this. Braslav clearly wanted to pay no less than the provisions were worth, but at the same time I knew he didn't want to end up feeling robbed. I joined in the argument a few times, supporting Braslav; I was, after all, the only other member of the party whose language was Serbo-Croat. Finally a price was agreed, and Braslav handed the money over, prudently not letting the peasants see exactly how much remained in his mixed bag of dollars, sovereigns and other currencies in gold coin.

After that we were invited a second time into the poor cottage where we had been received the day before. Again we stood and each drank a small glass of schnapps.

Then we said goodbye. 'If you are still stuck after two days,' one of the men said, 'Don't try coming back to us. We have spared you all the food and fuel that we could. There is another village about four miles north of the place where your train is. You will have to go there and beg.'

That speech gave us a bit of a jolt. At least it was honest. But it caused us to trudge away, out from the slush of the village street and back into the great snowfield that lay between us and our frozen express, in a sombre mood. As we began the walk, taking it in turns to pull the two sledges, none of us spoke.

Braslav...

It was barely twelve thirty. We were three hours ahead of where we had been yesterday at this stage of events. We should have been rejoicing over that, and over the sun that now shone full upon us from a clear blue sky, as well as the fact that we were laden with enough provisions to satisfy the hungriest of stomachs. But somehow a sense of foreboding hung over us. I at least, had a presentiment that, our outbound journey having gone so well, and the negotiations having ended so satisfactorily, all could not end happily. As indeed it did not.

Nedim...

Andrea saw them first. A small line of figures on the rim of a crest of snow, outlined against the snow-blue light. Andrea pointed without speaking. Braslav spoke, although almost in a whisper. 'They won't want us. They'll be after the sheep and goats. They'll already have smelt them. They're downwind of us.'

Roman spoke. 'If they do come close,' he said,

pulling his pistol from his pocket, 'they'll have this to reckon with.'

I said, 'Roman, have you ever shot a wolf?'

'Something like that,' he said, with a hint of evasion in his voice.

Having inevitably stopped for those few seconds we started again on our trek, though looking constantly back over our shoulders as if hypnotised by the sight behind us and by our own fear and dread.

For a full half minute the wolves remained immobile, standing proudly on their crest of snow like fanciful goblin ornaments on the ridge of a roof. Then they began to come after us.

It was impossible not to want to count them. They numbered eight. I had to ask Roman. 'How does your pistol work? How many bullets have you got?' I tried for a neutral, casual tone of voice, showing disinterested curiosity. Instead my shrill question merely gave away my state of near panic.

'Semi-automatic,' said Roman. 'Luger Parabellum. Swiss army issue. It reloads itself in under a second. The magazine has twenty rounds in it. Don't worry. I checked before coming out.' For some extraordinary reason I read into that last remark a veiled reproach of Braslav, though I said nothing about it.

How far away had they been when we first saw them? Half a mile perhaps? How long did it take them to narrow that gap enough for us to see clearly their long grey faces, their dark muzzles, their slanted eyes half-closed against the cold? Those short-long, long-short minutes were among the most uncountable of my life.

They did then what I had childishly been fearing most. They stopped a moment and howled at us. I felt my blood turn to ice-water in my veins, and my hair prickled between my scalp and cap. I wanted to hold Braslav but knew I couldn't. I wanted to know what Braslav was going to do about this new situation. I wanted to get inside his thoughts. That too I knew was impossible. Each of the five of us had to face this separately inside us. The wolves stopped howling now. Silently they charged at us.

Sacha was the first to react. He was nearest to the sledge that carried the logs. He picked one log up and threw it over-arm towards the middle of the pack. His throw was strong and his aim was good. The wolves had to swerve this way or that to avoid the missile, but it didn't deter them. They came on, bounding towards us. If you are starving, it went through my mind, you won't be deflected by a thrown lump of wood.

I heard the crack and whizz of Roman's bullet. I looked in hope for one of the wolves to fall dead but none of them did. A second later the first wolf reached the sledge on which lay the goats and sheep. Andrea had been dragging that sledge. Now he let go of the rope he was pulling it with as quickly as if it had turned to hot wire and staggered backwards towards us, stumbling and nearly falling as he came. Roman fired a second shot.

Then everything seemed to happen with an agonising slowness as happens sometimes in a dream. The leading wolf had hold of one of the sheep carcases and had started to drag it from the sledge. But then it lost power and stopped. It flopped belly-down into the snow, the sheep's muzzle no longer in its jaws. I realised that Roman's aim had been perfect this time. That wolf was dead.

The others seemed to take no notice of the fact. Five of them fell upon the sheep and goats on the sledge and sank their teeth into them and started to pull them off. Meanwhile the remaining two came past them, one on either side: they seemed to be carrying out a pincers movement towards us.

Roman fired another shot at the nearer of the approaching wolves, the one on our right, but nothing happened. Another shot came less than a second after it. It rang out at the same instant as Braslav gave a piercing shout. We turned. The other wolf had slipped past us on the left while all our attention was focused on the one Roman was trying to shoot, and it had somehow got hold of Braslav's leg. I was no more than two yards from this. I moved towards Braslav. Roman yelled at me, 'Stay back!' I did. Less than another second passed. Roman fired again and Braslav's wolf, wounded somewhere, succumbed to its own terror and turned and ran for it, giving vent to desolate howling as it went.

The wolf on our right now stopped and stared at us, uncertain what to do next. Roman fired at it again. This time he hit it in the head and to my astonishment it died in an instant, falling on its side in the spot where it had just stood.

Our courage returned to us. We ran towards the sledges, shouting, yelling at the wolves that were still struggling to get the sheep and goat carcases off. I hadn't counted Roman's bullets. I didn't think he'd used more than ten, though. At least I hoped he hadn't. There were five wolves left.

Seeing four men charging at them with loud ferocious whoops the wolves dropped their booty and backed off a foot or two. Roman didn't hesitate. Without pity he fired at each of them, at very short range. He killed two, while the last three, seeing they had no more hope of success, turned and ran for it, their tails lowered, across the endless snowy tract. They uttered howls of such limitless despair that they froze my heart. I thought how easily it might have been the other way around: that the sorrowful beasts running desperately across the frozen waste, bereft of food, companions and hope... It could have been the five of us ... or some of the five of us.

Roman shouted at me, 'For God's sake see to Braslav!'

Anger rose in me. 'Of course I'm seeing to Braslav!' I yelled back at him. 'Give us a chance!' I was already running the twenty paces back towards him. *Running!* With improvised snowshoes on my feet! In snow that was feet deep!

Braslav had fallen on his back, caught off balance by the suddenness of his wolf's attack. Only a few seconds had passed since then, but he was already back, if a little unsteadily, on his feet, and brushing the snow off.

'Are you in pain?' I asked, in dread of his answer. Horror was piling upon horror. I had no way of knowing how much worse everything would get.

'It doesn't hurt much now,' Braslav said. 'It was just a little nip. Like you get from a dog.'

'Did it draw blood?' I found I shouted that. If there was blood... Blood. A bite from a wolf... We all knew the stories about that. I fell at his feet and frantically started rolling the trouser-leg up above his boot. Two neat puncture wounds were there. A few beads of blood like ladybirds stood about. No blood was running. I supposed that was something to be grateful for, at least.

Sacha was kneeling in the snow beside me. 'I have iodine,' he said. He shoved a bottle under my nose. 'Put some on a hanky and dab it with it.' And, feeling like the most stupid and ill-prepared member of our party, or perhaps of the whole human race, I did exactly that.

FIFTEEN

Nedim…

Roman had just two bullets left. We resumed our trek. We guessed we'd come a mile when the wolves attacked. That left two miles ahead of us. And, despite the snowshoes, we were having a harder job than we'd had this morning, on account of the weight of the loaded sledges. Of course we all took turns to pull them, though now Braslav was exempt from this. He protested, but Roman and Sacha overruled him. He walked alongside me, and often with Andrea. More often than not it was Roman now who was striding out in front, whether he was dragging one of the sledges at the time or not.

After a time I noticed that Braslav was limping, and struggling along. I asked him if he wanted to stop. 'We can't stop,' he said. 'In this temperature that's dangerous.' But he did stop for a moment, just to catch his breath.

Roman turned and saw this. 'Sacha and I are all right with the sledges for a bit,' he said. 'Nedim, Andrea, put your arms through Braslav's and help him along.'

And so we staggered the second mile. It grew harder and harder, and Braslav seemed to be surrendering more and more of his weight to Andrea and myself. Suddenly I felt him go. He wasn't heavy but the unexpectedness of his faint brought Andrea and me crashing into the snow with him, the way coupled goods wagons derail when the one in front of them does.

Roman and Sacha dropped the reins of their sledges and came back. Together the four of us staggered with Braslav's body and placed him on top of the dead sheep and goats. By this time he had just about come to. We sat him up only long enough to give him a nip of brandy and some coffee (we had no water with us: we offered him a mouthful of snow but he shook his head) then we laid him back down on his still not quite cold woolly bed.

Now we set off two to a sledge. Roman and I, the two biggest of the party, harnessed ourselves to the now very heavy sledge that carried the dead animals and Braslav, while Andrea and Sacha shared the lighter weight of the sledge that bore the logs. There lay just a mile between us and the train, we reckoned, but it looked like being extremely tough.

Our spirits rose some ten minutes later, though, as the dark line of our train came into sight; the sun was sparkling on the snow on its roof. Ten minutes after that we had more cause for relief as we saw four figures heading out from the train across the snow towards us.

They reached us after a few more minutes. Two of them were conductors who had sat at our table last night, the other two were burly male passengers. Braslav got up at that point and said he would walk the last few hundred yards back. 'Oh no you won't,' said Roman, and physically lifted him back onto the sledge. We all gratefully accepted the offer of the new arrivals (kitted out with fruit-box snowshoes just like us) to pull the sledges on this last leg of the journey while we walked alongside, feeling that springiness of step that belongs to those who have just unburdened themselves of heavy luggage. Ten minutes later we were back at the train. Strangely enough, despite the dramas and dangers we had faced, and the terrible uncertainty that hung over Braslav's future health and chances of life, the return had none of the emotional nature of yesterday's. It was more like a normal homecoming from work. Routine, businesslike. And, while the passengers spilled out into the snow, laughing with relief at the sight of our laden sledges, approaching and examining the dead sheep and goats, from which Braslav was now disentangling himself and standing up, it was Andrea's voice that called out, routine and businesslike, 'Fetch the doctor for the driver. Urgently. He's been bitten by a wolf.'

'You're lucky I have the vaccine with me,' the doctor said. 'And that we've caught you quickly. Two hours ago only? You should be all right. But I'm afraid this has to go in the stomach. For a moment it will hurt a lot.'

We were seated in the restaurant car, the three of us. The doctor raised no objection to my presence. He might or might not have guessed that we were lovers. In any case the circumstances were so remote from normal civilian life that perhaps he felt that now, anything went. Or else he lazily assumed that driver and firemen went everywhere together, inseparable, like pepper and salt.

It did hurt. Braslav, stoic though he was, made a noise of pain through his clenched teeth that sounded like someone trying but failing to vomit. 'Sorry,' said the doctor, as Braslav doubled forward on his chair when the long needle came out. 'Sometimes we have to be cruel to be kind.' The doctor reached forward then and tousled Braslav's hair for an instant. That surprised me, though not unpleasantly. After all, Braslav had, without meaning to, practically laid his head in the doctor's lap. Then the doctor looked up at me as I stood beside them both. 'Take him somewhere he can lie down for a bit. Make him rest. Let him get some sleep. These last two days he's been through enough.'

'Yes he has,' I said with feeling. I, unlike the doctor, knew what had wounded him most.

Braslav...

Nobody likes to be dropped as team captain and replaced: that was what everybody always said. I had thought myself above such petty jealous feelings. Apparently I was not.

I could hardly find a gracious word to say to Nedim when, while I was still sore from the rabies injection, he wrapped blankets around me and left me to rest on the bottom bunk while he went off to do what he hadn't yet attended to – what *we* hadn't yet attended to – which was to rekindle the engine fire and build it up with the new supply of logs.

I fretted during the time he was away from me. I

wasn't used to it. We hadn't been out of sight of each other for four whole days now, or further than ten yards apart. Except for the few times when one of us had gone to use the toilet for five minutes. Even when our eyes had been closed in sleep we'd still kept in touch.

Now I wondered what he was doing minute by minute. I wondered if the fire had gone out. If he'd had trouble lighting it. If some of the pipes had frozen… Would he know what to do about that? He might have met other people along his twenty-yard way. The *chef de train* might have gone to the cab to talk to him. What would they have talked about? Would they have spoken about me and my misfortune? If so, what would they have said?

Nedim might take the opportunity, if he got the fire lit quickly, to wander down to the restaurant-car kitchen and have a chat there with the staff. With Roman, of course, who by now would be butchering goats and sheep ready for tonight's feast. With the conductors who had sat and swapped stories with us last night. With Andrea and the other pretty youths who waited table and prepared vegetables in the kitchen when they weren't doing that – or making snowshoes out of fruit boxes. He would be relaying tales of how his senior crewman had ended up risking the success of the day's expedition, and the lives of his comrades, because he'd been careless enough to get bitten by a wolf.

I lay awake waiting for Nedim and wondering about him for thirty-five minutes. I regularly checked my watch. It isn't too much to write that I pined for him.

Then suddenly the door opened and in he came. He looked at me, smiling at first, but then a look of dismay overcame his face. 'My darling, what's the matter?' he asked. He took three quick steps towards me, knelt beside the bunk, took my head in his hands and covered my warm face with kisses from his now-cold lips. 'My darling,' he repeated, 'are you all right?'

I locked my arms around his shoulders in an instant. So tightly that I could hear the breath I squeezed inside him coming out. I couldn't say anything to him. I broke down and wept against his cheek.

Nedim…

We just lay together and talked. Both of us beneath the same blanket; me with all my clothes on still – even my coat. Braslav had somehow convinced himself that I now cared more for Roman than I did for him. Two days ago it had been Andrea he'd been worried about.

'That's absurd, Braslav,' I told him. 'Roman?! Nobody's ever going to replace you in my affections, but if anyone was going to the last person in the world would be Roman.'

He asked me what I'd been doing since we'd spoken last. I told him I'd got the fire re-lit and piled logs on it. I'd checked for frozen pipes exactly as I'd seen him do yesterday. Doing all that had taken thirty minutes. Had I spoken to anyone? he wanted to know. Been to the restaurant car?

'No,' I said. 'Think about it. To get to the restaurant

car I'd have had to walk past the door to this compartment. Do you imagine I'd have done that? That I wouldn't have at least put my head round the door to see if you were asleep or awake. And even if you'd been asleep...' I began to get upset. I tried to imagine what I'd have done if Braslav had been asleep. Would I have left him and gone to talk to someone else? I wasn't sure, but I didn't think I would.

A knock sounded at the door. I answered. 'Who is it?'

'Andrea,' said Andrea's voice.

'Come in,' I answered.

If Andrea was surprised to have been invited into a compartment where two men lay wrapped together in a blanket on the same bed he showed no sign of it. Instead he said, 'You look very sweet, the two of you. Very cosy, very happy and very nice. Braslav, how are you feeling? The doctor says you've had a lucky escape.'

'He's feeling fine,' I said, speaking before Braslav could get the words out, in case using his voice might make him cry again. Um...'

'Yes, I came to tell you about that,' he said, reading – because sharing – my hunger-driven thoughts. 'The goat and mutton won't be ready before eight. It's only just been slaughtered so is tough and will take time to cook. But Roman is serving cabbage and potato soup in an hour from now. The passengers are already queuing up for it.'

'All right for us to queue up for it in bed?' I asked, and Andrea sniggered at that.

'One other thing… The *chef de train* asked for news about the engine fire. Is it still alight? The new logs? Frozen pipes…?'

I told him everything I knew about those subjects, exactly as I had told Braslav. Then Andrea went, and we did as I had suggested: spent the next hour together in bed; though as the hour unfolded we became a bit less fully dressed.

Braslav…

We went out in search of our cabbage soup, following our noses, queuing down the corridor towards the restaurant car among the passengers, like destitute people queuing at a soup kitchen. But actually, that was exactly our state. The destitute are separated from money only by circumstance, time and space. The same went for even the wealthiest of that dishevelled queue huddling, just like Nedim and me, in overcoats.

At last we arrived at the front of the queue and got our bowls of soup. Nedim and I had a word about this between desperate spoonfuls. Heaven is neither umpteen virgins nor angels playing harps. When you are as hungry as we were, Muslim or Catholic, Heaven is a bowl of cabbage soup. No more, no less. Then, without even checking the firebox, we went back to bed, where we stayed until – according to the timetable Andrea had given us – our goats would be cooked.

Nedim...

It was more than a feast. It was a celebration, a party, a return to life. It was only two days since we had eaten a full Orient Express banquet. But we had had nothing in between except last night's slivers of chicken, egg and bread, and so that memory, although so recent, seemed to belong to another life. Some of the passengers had spent most of the intervening hours wrapped up in their warmest clothes in their bunks, and who could blame them? Braslav and I had done the same as soon as we'd had the chance. But Braslav and I, along with Roman and Sacha and Andrea, had spent many of those hours wading through deep snow in the perishing cold. Though all were hungry, we were surely hungrier than most.

It was a simple stew of mutton, potatoes and goat. Roman had somehow found a couple of onions and carrots – chopped very small in order to go round – to flavour it with. I wondered if Roman had hidden the onion and the carrot along with the brandy, thinking ahead to possible emergency use. The thought of Roman and his talent for thinking ahead made me frown involuntarily. Braslav noticed that and asked me what I was thinking about. To be kind, and not wanting to complicate things, I said what was not the exact truth. It was a tiny thing but I was aware of it because it was the first time I'd ever done that to Braslav.

'I was thinking about the brandy that got stolen last night,' I said. 'I wonder who could have done that.'

'Well,' said Braslav, 'for all we know there's still a

murderer on board. We may as well also have a thief.'

'In a way,' I said, 'the small theft seems almost worse. A murder can be committed in hot blood, almost by accident, the way one shoots a wolf. But to steal a bottle of brandy from the community of people you've come to belong to... When you're all in the same boat...'

Braslav nodded his head. While it struck me that sin was in the eye of the beholder. There were two pairs of men on board – two that we knew about – who had sex with each other, in defiance of all their religions' precepts. In the hierarchy of sins, where murder and the theft of a bottle of brandy ranked, where would the passengers and other staff – people from all walks of life, nations and religion – place what Braslav and I now routinely did in bed, and hoped to do again once dinner was finished?

Roman was in the restaurant car now, walking among the tables, accepting the plaudits of the seated passengers. I wanted to add mine to theirs. I had been genuinely impressed by his courage, his shooting skill and his cool head earlier. I hung back for a moment, Others were speaking. Then Roman, who hadn't noticed me sitting nearby, said, laughing in reply to something that had been said, 'Yes. It takes a real man to face down and shoot a wolf.'

I felt like a child does when someone stubs a cigarette out on his rubber balloon. My dismay and disillusion were only out-topped by my desperate hope that Braslav hadn't heard Roman's remark.

SIXTEEN

Braslav...

As the convivial meal went on we learnt that we were not the only people who had been busy that day. Something had changed over the past two days. It was as if war had been declared and everyone had been called up. There were no distinctions now between passengers and staff, let alone between First-Class passengers and Second- or Third-Class.

During that day the *chef de train* had called the passengers together and, with their full agreement, organised them into teams that willy-nilly involved doctors, detectives and maybe-criminals alike, to clean the train. The task had included cleaning the filthy toilets and, following the example set by Nedim and myself, unfreezing the outflows underneath. As the temperature had risen somewhat that proved easier this third time around: a few rags soaked in paraffin and set alight had done the trick and, so far as anyone was saying, nobody had got showered with filth. A few buckets of snow had even been melted on the kitchen range and tipped into our tender tank.

I enjoyed a couple of glasses of wine with dinner, along with most of the others, although Nedim rather carefully abstained that night. During the meal I overheard Roman saying something about real men and wolves. I wasn't hurt by this: the remark was beneath contempt, and as far as I was concerned it put Roman in the same case. But I was glad that Nedim hadn't heard it. He would have been terribly upset.

Nedim...

Braslav insisted on coming with me to put the fire to bed, walking through the churned snow beside the tender, across what was left of the duck-board path. I had told him I could easily manage this on my own, and would have preferred him to go straight to bed and wait for me there. But no...

The penny dropped while we were putting a few last logs on. Braslav didn't just want to help me in a practical kind of way. He wanted to make up for what he must have seen as his failure during the return half of our day's trek. That and ... yes, there was another thing, I realised. He loved me so much that he didn't want to let me out of his sight. Even better than the doctor's pronouncement that Braslav wouldn't die of rabies, that realisation was the best thing that happened to me that day.

We were in a serious mood when we got to bed. Though not too serious to find we had erections when we undressed each other. Not too serious to lightly fondle them, and to want to make love. But Braslav found he wanted to say something first. 'I let you down today.'

'You didn't,' I said. 'You got bitten by a wolf. It could happen to anyone. I let you down last night, come to that. Getting drunk, passing out, no good to you for sex… And today was even worse. I didn't spot the wolf come past me and go for you…' I realised as I spoke that that had been the moment of all moments for me to be Braslav's protector, and I'd failed utterly. I heard myself choke up.

'It doesn't matter,' said Braslav. I felt him stroke my hair and felt and smelt his sweet alcohol-laden breath. I couldn't see him. It was so cold in the compartment that we'd pulled the blankets up over our heads when we got into the bunk.

I understood something at that moment. 'Then neither does anything else matter,' I said. 'We can't be perfect for each other every second of every day. We can't always be in the right place at the right time, supporting each other and up so close we can hear the other's heart beat.'

Braslav sighed. 'I know that,' he said. 'I just didn't know that you knew that. I've been pretending this wasn't true but – if we live long enough to survive this experience, if rescue comes and we get back to Belgrade – we may have to support each other from a distance.'

'Not too great a distance,' I said, like a girl again, or a spoilt kid. Sometimes I just couldn't help myself.

'If the distance becomes too great, and if it hurts too much, we'll shorten it,' Braslav said, and nibbled at my ear with his teeth and lips.'

'How will we do that?' I asked, sleepily now, not

161

really expecting an answer.

'Love will find a way,' Braslav said. 'It always does.'

'Yes,' I said. I didn't know that from experience, though. Neither could Braslav know, I thought. He hadn't been in love before we met either, not properly in love. That's what he'd said and I believed him. But I too knew the expression. 'Love will find a way.' It was something my father used to say, I now remembered. I didn't tell Braslav that.

Braslav...

In the morning we got up.

How obvious that is!

My father, during the short periods I knew him, used to say, 'The obvious is an unturned stone. Pick it up and look beneath it.'

I'm not sure I can do that. I'm not sure even what he meant. All I can do is to try and record faithfully that morning's events, as I've tried to record those of the few days that came before it.

We went to the restaurant car and queued for a small cup of black coffee. So did everybody else. There would be no breakfast this morning. Every one of us knew that. Nobody said it. There would be no lunch either. There would be another stew of goat and mutton this evening at six o'clock. Nobody announced that. The information somehow spread by whisper. As we arrived at the front of the coffee queue, there was Roman, standing with folded arms in the doorway of the kitchen. Anyone who wanted to break ranks and demand food before six this evening would have to get past him, his whole big body said.

I thought that was fair enough. I also knew that Roman had spent a second night on the divan in the corridor, enabling Sacha to spend a second night with Andrea. We had seen him there when we returned from bedding the engine's fire down and were going towards our own shared bed. I still had to respect Roman for that. I had thought all my life that you were free to like or dislike someone without examining the reasons for that like or dislike. Today I discovered that you were not. Things were a hundred times more complex than I'd thought.

Together Nedim and I walked round to the loco's cab. It had become a routine walk. Emergency conditions became routine things very quickly, I was discovering. We reawakened the fire and piled logs onto it. Then we looked into the tender tank. Seeing nothing below in the darkness us we dipped it. There was barely a foot of water in it, covered with a skin of ice.

'We need to get something in there,' I told Nedim. 'Just a bit. Enough to get us through the day at least.'

'We'll get help,' Nedim said. 'Forty people got the train cleaned yesterday and got the toilets unblocked. Some of them should surely be prepared to help gather snow and melt it and tip it into the tank.'

So we went and found the *chef de train* and he organised a chain gang to help us.

Nedim...

We were a team of sixteen, working in sunshine and rising temperatures. How much more quickly it all went than three days ago when there had just been the three of us – myself, Andrea and Braslav. The only thing that slowed us down now was the time it took to melt the snow buckets in the firebox. Low fire, logs not coal... But we kept at it. A quiet little passenger was among the team. I noticed his coal-dark eyes and carefully waxed moustache. I asked him his nationality, in a conversational way. He was from Belgium, he said. Apart from that he said not a word to anyone, though he scooped up snow and passed buckets along as energetically, if not more so, than anybody else.

Watching the line of passengers and crew obediently passing buckets along made me think of the poem by Goethe, *Der Zauberlehrling*, in which the half-trained apprentice of a sorcerer uses a spell to make his master's broom carry buckets of water for him. It all goes horribly wrong, of course. Eventually...

'Hey, look!' Andrea yelled suddenly at the top of his voice, standing on top of the tender tank. He pointed ahead of the train. He sounded overcome. 'Just look!'

I scrambled to join him on the tender top. So did Braslav. The rest stopped what they were doing and looked desperately up at us, waiting for news of any sort.

In the distance, across the snowy white, two upright plumes of black and white smoke were visible. They were not village chimneys, but something more powerful than that. 'What's that?' Andrea asked.

'I'd say they were two steam engines come to rescue us,' said Braslav laconically. 'What would be your guess?'

Braslav...

Anyone who lives in flat country knows how slowly the smoke of a train, let alone the dust kicked up by a horse and cart, approaches. But none of us had ever before watched a train approach at such a snail's pace. Nor had we watched the spectacle with such agonising mental thirst.

Andrea saw those plumes of smoke at nine o'clock. It was midday before they reached us. Long before that we realised what was happening. The double-headed train, travelling at best at a walking pace, was constantly being brought to a halt by deep snow and having to back up in order to charge the drifts.

In fact it wasn't the snow-plough that arrived first, but a number of soldiers in motorised sledges. Their arrival caused a great outpouring of joy from the passengers. Some deserted our chain-gang to go and welcome them. Others, to their credit, stayed at their posts, the little Belgian with the waxed moustache among them.

Eventually the army train came hissing to a stop, having burrowed its way through the drift that had trapped us for four nights, just a few feet from 72619's front buffer beam. A few feet, but those few feet were a wall of ice... Yet, after a few minutes, with many soldiers and many pick-axes...

Suddenly I was back at work. The snow-plough attached to the leading locomotive of the rescue train had couplings at the front, hidden beneath a sliding hatch (thank heaven, or it would have been no help to us) and was quickly attached to 72619. Almost as importantly, the steam pipe was also attached. Warmth would again be flowing around the carriages of our train, thanks to a power source that was bigger than our little log fire of the last two days.

Military shovels dug around the wheels of engine and train. The army wagons behind the two rescue engines had disgorged two hundred fit and energetic men. After three hours of work it was agreed between the army captain, the *chef de train* and me that we would give the train an experimental tug. If this went well the snow-plough train would reverse slowly all the way to Brod, towing us.

It didn't go well at first. Our train would not be moved. The brakes were frozen solid, locked on as I had left them when we hit the drift. Patiently the army detachment lit fires with oiled rags under each set of brakes: engine, tender, and every one of the carriages. Then we tried again. Nedim and I stood in the cab of 72619, though there was little for us to do there. We had no coal so could not get steam up and could not help with the tow. We just had to be pulled ignominiously, warming our hands from time to time in front of the cinders of what remained of our log fire.

Nedim...

What did we leave behind when we so unceremoniously left that nowhere place? Some duckboards lying in snow. Some piles of frozen human excrement. Other discards and wastes. The place itself would soon cease to be, anyway, its identity irrevocably lost, as most of it was composed of a transient snowdrift. So what remained? Memories of an ordeal, which would never leave any of us. People say that ghosts appear where people have left powerful memories behind them. If that is true, then that featureless stretch of track – which I never managed to recognise again when passing it at speed in normal conditions, devoid of snow – must be peopled by no end of ghosts. Perhaps those ghosts – the ghosts of all our memories of that place – will howl at night and be mistaken for wolves by nervous folk.

We had inspected the army train with interest. It consisted of six wagons as well as the two locomotives, and was equipped with a snowplough on the back, to help us through any blown snow that might have accumulated between the train's outward journey and our crablike return to Brod.

There wasn't a snow-plough stationed at Brod, we learnt. Our rescue train had come all the way from Zagreb. It had taken days. Though news of our disappearance had spread quickly the extreme weather, which now covered most of Europe, had hampered rescue efforts. And the army had had to deal with many other situations of equal desperateness.

Twenty-four miles lay between our enforced stopping place and Brod. It took two hours that winter afternoon, with our towing engines going backwards and the guard at the rear looking out for drifts. We didn't care. We were being rescued. And yet... and yet... There was a question in Braslav's eyes that I saw every time I looked there. And he read the same question in mine. Neither of us voiced it. Yet it was obviously the same question. It was, Where are we going to sleep tonight – and will we be able to share a bed when we get to wherever it is?

We didn't say much, watching the snowy landscape pass on either side of us, but alternately peered out through the lookouts till our ears felt like freezing, and warmed ourselves by the open fire-hole against the faint heat of our little logs.

Around us the white waste began to turn gold, blue and orange as the sun sank. At last it came peering sideways into the cab and lit us. It picked out the regulator and the steam pipes, the brake cylinders and the cut-off wheel. It shone into the firebox and, as the superstition goes, it 'put the fire out'. From time to time during those two hours Braslav and I seized the opportunity and each other's ears, and exchanged a cold kiss, away from the forward lookout portholes, which could have been glanced through by the rescue train's footplate team when they looked behind them. It was the least, but also the most we could do. We didn't know when our next chance would come. We didn't know what would happen next to us when, at six o'clock that evening we rolled, with long squeals of brakes, and wheels on sharp curves, into platform number three at Brod, the better part of a week late.

SEVENTEEN

Braslav...

Perhaps I had been expecting to see the platform crowded with people, waving and cheering our arrival. Something like the scenes I'd seen on kino newsreels of warships being welcomed back to their home port. But there was nothing like that. I shouldn't have been disappointed, but somehow I was.

But of course people don't wait five days for a train that hasn't shown up. They catch other trains, find other routes. Two other Orient Expresses had arrived at Brod from the north in the intervening days; the engines had been turned, and they had taken the carriages, with northbound passengers aboard them, back towards Paris.

So only a handful of people were waiting for us on the platform. And they were far from pleased to be told that the engine had to be uncoupled, towed to the yard, coaled and watered and checked over, the fire re-lit with coal, not logs; and that it would then take a good few hours to get steam up. Even if all was well with 72619 we would not be leaving Brod till midnight at the earliest.

The *chef de train* asked us if we would be able to cope with all that. We had been up for eight hours already, and were now being asked to stay awake for a further eight even before we set off on the nearly ten-hour haul to Trieste. We were about to say a brave but foolish yes to that – we didn't want to be parted from 72619 at this stage and … well, it was obvious to me at least, Nedim and I didn't want our astonishing adventure together to come to an end just yet.

But I was saved from having to say it. The station master arrived and told us that a shunt driver and fireman from the yard would see to the coaling and firing-up and would return the engine to the platform when steam was up, all being well, around midnight

'In which case,' said the *chef de train*, 'I suppose we can let you keep your compartment in the Athens-Paris coach for a few more hours, given the exceptional circumstances. Let you get some sleep.' He said the last bit without any trace of irony or suggestiveness. Perhaps he still hadn't guessed, or been told, about us. If he hadn't been told, then it was Roman who hadn't told him. Perhaps there were things I had to thank Roman for yet.

Nedim…

Steam engines don't have keys the way motor-cars do. But when we handed 72619 over to the shunt crew and watched her being towed away across the snowy points I had the feeling I imagined a motorist might have when he hands the keys of his precious vehicle over to the stranger who will overhaul it. I watched our loco trundling slowly away until she was hidden from sight by a row of carriage sheds, and found myself looking forward hopefully to the moment of her reversing back into the platform with steam up.

'Stop daydreaming,' I heard Braslav saying. 'Let's get you inside and into bed.' Since vacating our engine cab we were standing side by side on the platform. I followed him into the Athens-Paris coach.

It was warm inside! I had almost forgotten the meaning of warmth. In fact the compartment felt positively hot. But it was also very definitely the last time we would see the interior of an Orient-Express compartment, with its monogrammed sheets, inlaid wood panelling and Lalique glass. Unless, by some weird chance that was unlikelier than anything in the Thousand and One Nights, we should at some future date become astonishingly rich.

We were determined to make the most of this short time that was left to us: our last few hours in a First-Class Orient Express compartment and bunk. We began by stripping each other's clothes off – something we hadn't done completely for two days now – and rolling exuberantly together, naked on the carpet.

After a little while Andrea knocked at the door (by now we recognised his way of knocking) and, without attempting to come in, told us there were bowls of goat stew and a glass of wine each on a tray outside in the corridor. We hadn't been able to secure major food supplies at Brod, he told us through the closed door, but at least the *contrôleur* had managed to replenish the wine stocks and there would be croissants and butter for breakfast as well as milk for the coffee. 'I'll save you some,' he said very sweetly, 'and bring it round to the cab at the first morning stop. And by the way, you'll be pleased to know they've taken the corpse of the murdered man out of the refrigerator van and sent it to the town mortuary.' We told him we were pleased to hear that.

We waited till Andrea's footsteps had died away and then I darted out into the corridor to retrieve the tray of supper. My heart missed a beat at the sight of the Compagnie director standing at the far end of the corridor, looking out of the window and smoking a cigarette. He must have seen my naked dash out and back again, but was clearly going to pretend he hadn't.

We ate our stew sitting on the edge of our bunk, decadently naked, then climbed together into it... And promptly fell asleep in each other's arms until Sacha's discreet knock awoke us. Our engine was in sight, he told us, backing down the track towards us, with steam up...

We had last stood together in the cab of a moving train almost exactly four days ago. Then we had stopped as abruptly as a clock, shortly after midnight. Now, almost as abruptly we started off again, shortly after midnight, as the station master raised his green lamp, giving us permission to pull out of Brod.

How sweet it was to hear again that deep chuff of the exhaust as it escaped through the smoke-box. How reassuring the roar of the blaze in the firebox as it was pulled by that very exhaust faster and faster into the heating tubes. As we gathered power the white smoke pumping from the funnel ahead of us turned red with the glow of the flames that licked through the boiler tubes and into the smoke-box. Bright red sparks flew up amidst the escaping smoke and steam like djinns released from bottles or lamps. How reassuringly familiar it was, how reassuring it was to be back at work with Braslav. As reassuring as the reawakened ticking of a stopped clock or watch.

And yet all was now completely different. The clock had started again, certainly, but it had not turned back. Monumental things had happened to Braslav and me in the intervening days. We were not the same people we had been when the train ploughed into the snowdrift. We had been tested by fire, cold, hunger, deprivation, shared terror and sheer physical endurance in snow and ice. We had also been transformed utterly – never to be the same again whatever might happen to us – by our first (and I privately hoped, only ever) experience of falling in love.

So we rode the footplate together through the remainder of that night. As we stood at our respective front lookouts, from time to time I would feel Braslav's gloved hand reach for mine around the regulator handle, and I would clasp his, and we would stay like that for perhaps a minute or more, until the need for me to add coal to the fire or for Braslav to adjust the regulator or the cut-off caused us to release our fond grip. I wondered at those moments of riding the rails hand in hand with Braslav how many drivers and firemen, in the hundred-year history of railways, had ever done this. The answer was, of course, mind-bogglingly impossible to guess.

In darkness we followed the river Sava upstream in its wide plain towards Zagreb, our lonely headlight picking out the pencil lines of the rails through the snow ahead of us. Then little by little the snowfields on either side of us came into sight, shining an eerie blue as the sky behind and to the right of us began to lose the opacity of night. By the time we reached Zagreb and pulled into the platform there the sun was touching the peaks of the mountains ahead of us even while the city around us was still bathed in pre-dawn's ghostly twilight.

There were few passengers awaiting us at Zagreb, although a few of ours got out there. We were more or less unexpected: hours early or days late depending which way you looked at it. We were following no timetable on our way to Trieste. Just getting there was the object of our trip.

It gave me a jolt to see and hear Andrea on the platform at the entrance to the cab. 'I've brought you the breakfast I promised,' he said. He handed it up: a paper bag containing a Thermos and two cups, a screw of sugar and four hot, buttered croissants.

'Step up here a moment,' Braslav said, and Andrea did. 'This is what the place looks like when we're warm and running,' Braslav said. He showed the cab off quite proudly, as though it were a house he'd just bought, pointing out the regulator, brakes, cut-off and gauges almost as if he'd invented those controls himself. Surely Andrea must have seen all this before, I thought, yet

Andrea played along and politely allowed himself to be impressed.

Andrea only stayed a minute; he had to get back. As he was leaving, though, Braslav put an arm out and drew Andrea to him, then kissed him lightly on the cheek. Not to be outdone I quickly followed suit, then Andrea stepped backwards out of the cab and down onto the platform, then disappeared from sight behind the tender as he walked back to his work.

Two days ago, I couldn't help thinking, Braslav would not have done that – kissed Andrea, I mean – and I wouldn't have dared to in front of Braslav. What had changed? I wondered. Did it have something to do with Braslav's growing confidence in the solidity of *us?*

We set off again. The mountains ahead of us were now fully sunlit, though still covered with the snow's blue and white coat. Our way looked ready to smash us into the mountains' sides, but a few miles before that we curved off to the left, still following the Sava upstream, but now through narrow valleys with steep slopes on either side. We left Croatia and entered Slovenia, though – hush – we were supposed to call the whole place Yugoslavia these days, and we wound our way steadily upward to our next stop, Ljubljana, which we reached around nine o'clock.

I had never been so far from home before. The spires and domes of Ljubljana looked foreign and exotic; I was excited by the sight. I heard myself blurt out to Braslav, 'I want to travel with you. I want to come to places like this with you. See other places. France, Germany America…' Hearing myself say that I felt like the biggest ever idiot. I was astonished to hear Braslav say, in a very charged voice, 'I'd like that too. With you. Just us. I'd like that more than anything in the world.' Then he pulled me away to the side of the cab that was furthest away from any eyes on the platform, and reached around me and gave me a kiss.

'Braslav,' I said. 'Can I…? When we leave the platform in a minute, can I be the one to pull the whistle chain? Would you let me do that?'

Braslav roared with laughter. 'Of course you can,' he said. 'You need to give it a bloody strong tug, though, or it doesn't work.'

A moment later the signals came from the *chef de train* and the station master on the platform. 'Now,' said Braslav.

I pulled down on the whistle chain with all my might. The whistle roared and shrieked. 'Can I do it again?' I asked, suddenly high with excitement.

'Of course,' said Braslav, laughing. Again I yanked the chain… And the chain broke. Both of us were doubled up with laughter as Braslav eased the regulator open. I was having more fun, I thought, than I'd ever had before in my life.

We climbed steeply after Ljubljana, winding a

crooked way between two mountain ranges towards a high pass. I had never seen anything like it. Pine trees grew in infinite number, somehow keeping their footing on the perilously steep slopes. Each one wore its own snowy hood. Every bend we rounded produced yet more mountains, each one surpassing the previous ones in height. I kept stopping and looking out at these heart-stopping sights, speechless and open-mouthed. Only with an effort did I remind myself each time that we needed extra steam for the climb and that I was still at work and must shovel and sweat more than ever in order to keep the fire up. Braslav was enjoying his new role as tourist guide, I noticed. He told me with the pride of one who knew his geography that the mountains that towered to the right of us were the south-easternmost edge of the great range of the Alps. I wanted Braslav to be my guide for ever. I would travel the world with him till the end of our life.

The work involved in climbing towards a mountain pass has its reward, I discovered. As we reached the top of our climb, Braslav closed the regulator, turned to me and smiled. 'Relax for a bit. Enjoy the ride. Just watch for signals and let gravity do the rest.'

There was still a bit of work to be done: gravity didn't do quite all of it. The fire still needed making up lightly every few minutes. Braslav had to apply the brakes often and fiercely on the mountain curves, and the wheels shrieked tooth-achingly as their flanges bit into the rails on the tight corners. 'All downhill to Trieste,' Braslav said. There was one last stop among the mountains, at a small town called Postojna. Here the border police came aboard. They would stay on the train all the way to Trieste, Braslav said, going down the train, checking visas, passports and other documents. But they began with us, climbing into the cab and checking the papers the Compagnie had given us. They examined them minutely, stamped them, and then climbed down again. 'Thank you,' they said, and exchanged a curt little bow with us.

After we had set off from Postojna the air grew warmer, and a new bright light came into the sky ahead. I felt as though I were setting out on a foreign holiday... I who had never had a holiday of any sort. 'You'll see it in a few minutes,' Braslav said.

'See what?' I asked.

'When you see it you'll know what it is.'

Like a child expecting a present, I found I already half knew what it would be. Then it came into view as we rounded yet another sharp curve. I had never seen it before, of course. I hadn't expected, somehow, that it would be so luminously beautiful, or that it would be so big. It was blue and green, and it sparkled in the morning sun like broken glass. It lit the sky above it, and the sky above it gave it light. I felt my chest shaking with the shocking wonder of it. Then I felt Braslav's arm around my shoulder. I put my hand over his hand as it lay across my chest, and neither of us could speak.

EIGHTEEN

Nedim…

Sacha had said that all rail routes through Europe converged on Trieste. That was elegant and poetic and perhaps true in the bigger sense. In the smaller sense, though, it wasn't like that. The routes might well have converged but the rails did not. Because of what I have learned to call topography the main railway lines between Italy and Yugoslavia bypass the seaside city, and the city centre is reached by a ten-mile spur of track. Our way from Ljubljana brought us to the top of a high escarpment a few miles from the sea, with an awe-inspiring view down to Trieste far below. It then ran some miles away from Trieste before a sharp loop brought us down the steep slope at a point where the gradient was manageable, and then doubled back onto the spur, which ran almost along the beach. All in one morning I had had my first sight not only of mountains but also of the sea. I marvelled at the fact that Braslav had been doing this journey two or three times a week for several years. He had these views, these images of sea and mountains already stored in his head. You would think that store of visual impressions would have made a huge difference to his personality, but that didn't seem to be the case. I wondered if I would be a changed person after today as a result of seeing all this. As I had been changed, and Braslav too, by the experience of falling in love. I wanted to talk to him about this at some point, though perhaps now – coasting along the shore into Trieste, with the sea wind singing in my ears and the sun sparkling up at me from the silver water of the Mediterranean – was not the moment for it.

In contrast to our low-key arrival in Zagreb there was something triumphal about our entry into Trieste. It was later in the morning, for a start, and people had had longer notice, by telegraph, of our progress. The platforms of the terminus station were crowded with sight-seers. Cameras were raised high above people's heads and shutters clicked and flashed. Braslav had no sooner brought the train to an impeccably smooth stop three feet from the buffers than a horde of people were at the entrance to the cab, cameras flashing in our faces, and voices asking in Italian, German and English, for us to give them our exclusive story. Neither Braslav nor I had been expecting this. We were taken aback by the situation and unsure how to handle it.

Luckily Braslav saw someone he knew at that moment, shouldering his way through the crowd towards us. Braslav pointed to him. 'The Compagnie's Trieste agent,' he said. 'He'll sort this out.'

Which he then did. He told the reporters there would be a proper press conference in fifteen minutes, and told them in which part of the station it would be held. 'Till then, please give these fellows a chance to breathe and get cleaned up.' But the photographers continued to snap away at my coal-grimed face, afraid perhaps that some of the magic of the adventure would be lost once I'd washed it.

The agent then turned his back on the press-men and talked to us. 'The schedule is all out of joint,' he said. 'We plan to get it back on track tomorrow, with a south-bound Express leaving Paris in the morning. You can pick it up at six tomorrow evening and take it back to Belgrade overnight. As usual.' He addressed the last words to Braslav, whom he knew. Then he looked us both up and down. 'That is, if you're both fit enough.' We nodded and said yes. He said, 'Stay tonight in the *pensione*, of course.'

I had already done the calculation. We were being given the best part of two days in Trieste, as well as the night. I couldn't help grinning broadly at the thought of that.

Together with the platform crew we detached 72619 from the train of coaches. In an hour's time an Italian locomotive would be backed down onto the other end of the train, and, driven by an Italian crew, the Express would be hauled away north and westwards, on the Italian section of its long journey to Paris. Once the train had cleared the platform a shunt crew would run 72619 backwards to the engine yard where she would be sided until tomorrow when we picked her up, turned her on the table and brought her back. But now we had a press conference to face.

'Want a wash?' the agent asked us. Braslav said yes. I said that I'd like to give my armpits a rinse but would leave my face black for the press conference. I said I thought the reporters would rather like that. Braslav and the agent both laughed but they saw the point.

The *chef de train* and the member of the Compagnie board said most at the press conference, which was held in the cramped space of the Compagnie agent's office. They spoke quickly, as the train would soon be ready to depart. Some of the passengers had tales to tell also, but about the murder not a word was said. It seemed there was some unspoken agreement not to bring the matter up.

Roman spoke up when it came to tell of the expeditions to find food, and the difficulties of feeding so many with so few and such unpromising ingredients. He was fluent in Italian as well as German, it turned out. Braslav answered a question or two in Serbo-Croat. He paid tribute to Roman's courage and skill in dealing with the wolves. That was big of him, I thought. It had been a matter of chance that Roman was equipped with a gun while we were not.

Then Roman surprised me by piping up and saying exactly that. He went on to praise Braslav's qualities as a team leader, getting us to the village in the first place and handling negotiations when we got there. Perhaps he had come to regret his boastful remark of two days before. Perhaps I'd misunderstood it. I didn't speak at all. But a good many photos were taken of my soot-black face. I was glad I'd had the forethought not to wash it.

Suddenly it was over. Braslav and I found ourselves saying goodbye to Sacha, Andrea, Roman and all the other train staff. They would be setting off for Paris, while we had our day or so of rest in Trieste. Their paths would cross with Braslav's again sometimes in the future. They might not cross with mine, though, and that sudden parting was a bit of a wrench. Especially parting with Andrea, I had to admit.

The Compagnie agent called us aside in the middle of these farewells on the platform. He put a hand on each of our shoulders. Then, nodding his head as he spoke, he said a bit stiffly, 'The Compagnie is very grateful for your courage, co-operation and hard work during the past week. Enjoy your time in Trieste.' He handed Braslav an envelope. 'You'll need some expenses while you're here.' He looked at me and said, 'Make sure he gives you half of it,' and then he winked.

Braslav...

The sum of money contained in the envelope was decidedly generous, we discovered when we opened it. I walked with Nedim through the little maze of streets near the station to the place where we drivers and firemen were normally put up. I knew the *pensione* well, though Nedim of course did not. It was fairly basic: a roof over one's head, a room with two bunk beds in it, a bathroom that was shared by everybody in the house.

The staff knew me, of course. They had heard about the snow-lost Orient Express and wanted to hear all about it. They treated us a bit like heroes, to be honest, and it gave me a thrill to be introducing Nedim as my workmate. I would have liked to be able proudly to present him as my lover, but of course I could not. The world was far from ready for that. I did wonder, though, whether perhaps the nature of our relationship wasn't blindingly obvious from the way we comported ourselves and the looks on our faces.

I asked at once if we could have a bath. At shortly before lunchtime it was an unusual time of day for such a thing, but the *pensione*'s staff clearly saw the point of it, and probably smelt the point of it too. We would have to wait twenty minutes, they told us, while the geyser heated the water up.

The lady of the establishment had a query then. We would want two baths, one a little later than the other, would we not? I was astonished to hear Nedim say with the smooth fluency of the practised liar (which Nedim was not) that one bath would do for the two of us: we were conscious of the need not to waste water and precious heat.

I took Nedim up to the room they had given us. It was one I'd had before. In the past I'd shared it with black-faced firemen who didn't matter to me very much. Now I was to share it with the black-faced fireman who mattered more than anyone or anything on earth. When we got inside the room we started kissing. We didn't stop until the knock came on the door to tell us that the water had heated up.

Inside the bathroom a surprise awaited us. There were

laid out two pairs of clean socks, two vests, two pairs of underpants, and a clean shirt each. 'I have two sons,' the woman said. 'Borrow these from them. Return them next time you come to Trieste.'

I hadn't shared a bath with anyone since I was a small child. Neither had Nedim, he said. Eagerly we undressed and gingerly we stepped into the six inches of water. By the time we were sitting knee to knee in the hot tub we were so excited by the novel experience that both our cocks were erect. We admired and touched each other's. 'Did you…' Nedim asked hesitantly '…when you were much younger, I mean … did you ever masturbate in the bath?'

'I still do, sometimes,' I admitted, feeling a bit sheepish.

Nedim laughed. 'So do I, actually. I wasn't going to admit that unless you did. But now you have.' After that the next thing was inevitable. We stood in the water, covered each other with soap, clasped each other tightly with one slippery hand and with the other hand did to each other exactly what we had just been talking about.

We stayed playing and cuddling in the water until it began to cool, then got out. We returned to our room wrapped in towels and carrying our clean and dirty clothes with us. Then we climbed naked together in between the clean smooth sheets of the lower bunk and, embracing each other, slept soundly till four o'clock.

It was still early February, but we were on the coast. The warm sea helped keep the temperature above freezing, the mountains inland had helped to keep the worst of that winter's ferocious weather, which had come from the north, away from Trieste. There was little snow in the streets, and what there was had shrunk and melted across the pavement since we arrived at midday.

I took Nedim out into the streets and we threaded our way towards the sea. I took him to the Caffè Tommaseo in the piazza of the same name, which glanced around a corner at the sea. I'd never been inside the place, just seen the outside of it, inhaled deeply the aroma of fiercely roasting coffee beans, and taken a look through the windows at the stylish interior as I walked past. The place had been 'too good for me' I'd thought cringingly, as well as too expensive.

Everything was changed now. Nothing could be too good for the new entity that was Nedim and me. *Us.* And thanks to the envelope our agent had given us, the Caffè Tommaseo was no longer out of our price range – at least, not for tonight. I led the way inside. There was a look on the face of the waiter we walked past that indicated he was unsure whether to let us in or throw us out. Before he could decide I led Nedim to a table, sat us both firmly down at it, then took the envelope of money out of my pocket, took a large denomination note out of it and slipped the corner of it under the glass vase of flowers that decked the table top. I then smiled broadly up at the waiter and he smiled back and made his decision and brought us the menu to look at. I knew that the gesture I had made would be regarded as common by rich folk. But when you're poor and need to show you're solvent you have no choice but to do things like that.

The coffee arrived in beautiful small cups. A little bowl accompanied them: it had whipped cream in it. Together we looked up at the room around us. The ceiling was highly decorated; there were plaster mouldings, there was gilt. 'It's like the Orient Express all over again,' I said.

'Hmmm,' said Nedim. 'I think I'm beginning to get used to this.' Then he said, 'If 'twere now to die…'

'…'Twere now to die most happy,' I finshed the quote. 'Where did you get that?'

'It's Shakespeare,' he said.

'I know that,' I said and realised I'd almost snapped that. I reached for his hand across the table and clasped it. More gently I said, 'I meant where did *you* get it? I've heard you quote Shakespeare before. And Goethe…' He was a simple fireman from a poor family in Bosnia for heaven's sake.

'From my father,' Nedim said, sounding a bit vulnerable as he said it.

'Ah,' I said, and decided to let the matter drop.

We walked by the sea. There were no beaches in the town centre, only docks. But still it was the sea and it was Nedim's first experience of it. I was so conscious of that fact and of how much it obviously meant to him that I found myself constantly on the edge of tears as we walked. I was looking at the familiar scenery as if through Nedim's eyes, seeing the sea as if for the first time, the way Nedim saw it. This had never happened to me before. I don't need to write down the reason for it. Reader, if you've ever been in love, or even if you haven't, you already know it.

Nedim…

Walking by the sea, at sunset and after, with a lover. A week ago I would never have dreamed of this. I walked a foot above the pavement. So did Braslav. I wasn't so innocent as to not know that.

We went to a bar beside the sea. Although it was cold now that night had fallen we sat out on the pavement like stupid tourists. We sat listening to something I had never heard before. It was like a steady breath. It came in with a little rasp of shingle on shingle, then went slowly out with a sigh that was a thousand feet deep. It was the huge, quiet sound of the biggest thing on the face of the earth. I might have never heard it before. I might never hear it again. But I knew the sound was as old as the world was. It had been going when Abraham was a boy, was an old sound by the time of the birth of the Prophet. It would still be going, rasping in and sighing out, a million years after Braslav and I were dead.

'Why are you crying, little one?' Braslav suddenly said.

'I'm not crying,' I told him, startled. 'And I'm not your little one. I'm four inches taller than you are. And double your muscle-weight.'

Braslav gave me a smile I shall never forget. 'You're still my little one,' he said in a whisper. He stood up. 'Come now. Let's get ourselves something to eat.'

NINETEEN

Nedim…

Braslav knew where all the best restaurants were. He'd just never been inside them before, having never had the money. Now he marched us confidently up to one of the better places in town, only for us to be told at the door, with a smile but quite firmly, that we wouldn't be let in if we weren't wearing ties. For answer Braslav produced his envelope of money and showed a couple of the notes that were inside it.

'You could buy yourselves a pair of ties,' the head waiter said, 'and still have plenty left for a good meal.'

Braslav hesitated a second, then he said, 'I've another idea. We'll be back in half an hour. Keep a table for us.'

He told me his idea as we walked away. It was perfectly simply. In ten minutes we were back at our digs. 'Your sons who kindly lent us their clothes,' Braslav said to the woman, 'do they have a couple of ties they could lend us just for the next couple of hours…?' Twenty minutes later we were back at the restaurant.

We had a bean and sauerkraut soup, and then a wonderfully fresh grilled sea-bass – straight from the Med. A bottle of the local terrano wine accompanied all this. It was all new and delicious; it was like dining yet one more evening on the Orient Express.

On the way back through the winding streets we occasionally passed pairs of half drunk sailors, walking with linked arms. I did the same to Braslav. 'Be careful,' he said. 'You'll get us arrested.'

'Not if we pretend to be a little more drunk that we are,' I said. I pretended to lurch a bit, and Braslav decided to ignore his cautious side and pretended to be propping me up. I sang a couple of Bosnian peasant songs to add a bit of what's called verisimilitude to the pretence. We didn't get arrested, and had great fun doing it, though out of prudence we dropped each other's arms as we crossed the threshold of the *pensione*; as we handed back our ties we pretended to be talking about the afternoon's football results.

That pretence too was quickly dropped once we got upstairs. Balancing precariously on our narrow bunk we made love – with me fucking Braslav and him coming on my tummy shortly afterwards – in the charged and urgent way of lovers who don't know when if ever they will again get to share a bed. Then we climbed in between the sheets and, holding each other warmly, slept the sleep of the just-had-sex.

Braslav...

We went to the office of the Compagnie agent, to reconfirm our departure schedule. The news was better than we expected. We were going to be spoilt, in the way traditionally accorded to returning heroes. We would not have to go to the engine yard early to collect our chariot, let alone spend the whole afternoon setting the fire and getting steam up. A team of local shunt men would see to that, and bring 72619 trundling back into the station, ready for us to drive off to Belgrade, just after sunset at six o'clock. Meanwhile, the agent asked us, had we seen the morning's papers yet? He showed us them. Our photos were all over them. Especial prominence was given to Nedim's grimy face. We left the office and took a local train two stops to a suburb called Barcola where we spent the rest of this mild February day on the beach. At one point, rather out of the blue, I asked Nedim what his father's name was. 'Ahmed,' he said.

Nedim...

Dusk was greying the air as we pulled out of Trieste. Someone had mended the whistle chain, and Braslav let me pull it again. This time I was more careful with it.

We steamed through Barcola, where we'd spent the day, after just a few minutes, then took the sharp turn that led away from the Trieste spur, and up the escarpment. Another right turn took us back along the main line above Trieste. It was dark by the time we found ourselves looking down over the city. The lights were on down there, and the city sparkled like a tray of jewels that were laid out on black velvet in the window of a shop. Far off were other twinkling lights that belonged to ships miles out at sea, and once or twice lighthouses unexpectedly flashed. Then the hillside hid the view from our sight and I wondered when, if ever, I would again see Trieste.

How quickly we seemed to retrace our steps. We

climbed into the Alpine pass. The halt at Postojna came and went. We were back in the realm of snow again, but, although the sleepers were hidden by the white blanket, the rails stood out clearly, uncovered, in front of our headlight. We stopped at Zagreb around the time the passengers would be settling down to dinner – it felt odd, suddenly, not to be sharing that experience, but we'd eaten well during the day at Barcola – and then we stopped again at Brod in the middle of the night.

Some time after leaving Brod we passed the place where we had spent four days and nights. Passed it without seeing it, not even spotting the remains of our snowdrift as we roared, spewing flames and sparks into the darkness, along the track. There was no sign of that unlucky place. With the drift ploughed away the location had literally ceased to exist... So pass the glories of the world. But also the bad things. The motto that makes you sad when you are happy and happy when you are sad, as the ancient story tells us, is none other than, "All things must pass."

We continued on, sailing across the plains of the Sava and then the Danube, to the Vinkovci stop. And then at last we steamed in through the Belgrade suburbs just as the night was turning grey again in the new day's first light.

Belgrade. Belgrade. Arriving there I felt my stomach sink. It wasn't my home, any more than it was Braslav's. It was the capital city of our disparate new country: the place to which we and a million others had migrated because we had to work. Belgrade. It was the place where Braslav and I lived in separate apartments: the place where I would today be separated from Braslav.

Braslav...

I wasn't going to let him go easily. I wasn't going to let him go, full stop. Having found the man I was created for, the person I was put on earth to love and cherish, I would never relinquish him. Not even for one night.

From close by the buffers in the terminus we watched the coaches of the Orient Express leave the platform, pulled, as usual, by a Bulgarian loco under the control of a Bulgarian footplate team, and shortly turn left towards the south as it accelerated. Then, when the lowered signal announced the line was clear for us, I opened the regulator a little and we began to chuff slowly – following the departing train a mile or two, though at a growing distance from it – towards the yard where Nedim and I both worked.

'Here's the plan,' I said. Nedim looked at me expectantly, eager, like a child who has been told he's going have a treat but doesn't know what it is yet. His relief at the mere thought that I might have a plan in mind was more than evident. I grinned at him and gave his lips a sudden impulsive kiss. I couldn't help it.

'We'll go and check our respective schedules,' I said. 'Together. I'm not letting you out of my sight. And, whatever the coming days hold for us in the way of work, we'll both be due for a rest period now. Probably a full day's sleep. And I'm still not letting you out of my sight. You're coming back to my place, poor and simple though it is. Into my room. That is where we're going to sleep. Let my apartment-mates think what they like.' I'd spent some time on the journey thinking about this. At first I'd been afraid I wouldn't be able to go through with it. I was deeply afraid of what other people might say – or even do – to us. But during the drive here from Trieste I seemed to have crossed some internal Rubicon. I wasn't afraid any more. Or if I was, then the mere existence of Nedim, his being by my side, cancelled that feeling completely out.

Nedim…

I loved that sudden flash from Braslav of decisiveness. He would sort the future out. With luck he might look after me for the rest of his life. We spoke to our two foremen about our schedules, catching them both in different corners of the shed. Then we compared notes. I was free now until five o'clock next morning; Braslav wouldn't be called back to work until four tomorrow afternoon. But whereas I would finish work tomorrow evening, Braslav would be away for two and a half days, including his stopover in Trieste. I didn't know how I was going to manage without him suddenly; life with no Braslav beside me now would be meaningless. And besides, I now discovered that I would be very envious of him, spending time in the spring sunshine without me on the Italian coast.

We walked through streets I knew less well than Braslav, to the place where he lived. He put an arm around my shoulder as we walked. 'Think of it as a start,' he said. 'We've got a place to sleep together at least. We've twenty hours before your next shift starts. Let's concentrate on that and make the most of it. All over the world there are millions of people in love who are having to spend more than just three days apart.'

'I know,' I said, trying not to sound downhearted. I looked around me at the grey and sunless streets of our poor quarter of Belgrade, and down at the grey and watery slush beneath our feet. 'It's just that you're going back to Trieste, without me,' I whinged. 'You'll be doing that twice a week or more for the rest of your working life, maybe. Leaving me here with this...' I kicked out at a pile of slush.

Braslav stopped walking and turned to face me. He put both his hands on my shoulders and looked hard into my eyes. 'Darling,' he said to me very firmly, 'without you with me I shall never enjoy being in Trieste. Your company has spoilt me completely. Whenever I'm there I shall long to be back here with you, and wonder what you are doing, minute by minute. Two days apart will hurt me just as much as it will you, but we have to live in the real world; we both have to work to earn a crust.'

'I'm sorry, darling,' I said, suddenly ashamed of my outburst. 'I was being selfish and not thinking straight.'

'It's all right, *Schätzchen,*' Braslav said. 'You had every reason to say what you did. We'll find a way to be together permanently eventually. I mean, I will find a way. That's a promise. We'll get there, make no mistake.'

'Thank you,' I said, and began to look forward to the kiss I would thank him with as soon as we had attained the privacy of his apartment.

Braslav...

I unlocked the door and in we went. One of my flat-mates, Sergej, was sitting in the kitchen drinking coffee. I realised the place must look an awful squalid mess. I took the bull by the horns and introduced Nedim. 'He's had a bit of a problem with his digs,' I lied to Sergej. 'He'll be sleeping on my floor for a bit.'

Sergej shook Nedim's hand. 'I know you by sight,' he said. 'Seen you in the mess canteen. You're on the saddle-tanks. At least you used to be. I've seen the papers this morning. So has everybody else. Hero of the Orient Express, you seem to be. Did they pay you well for the story?' Sergej's narrow eyes lit up at the thought of that.

'Not a penny,' I put in hastily. 'Though we got an expenses-paid evening in Trieste, courtesy of the Compagnie Internationale des Wagons-Lits. Anyway, we've just driven here through the night, so excuse us if we head upstairs and catch up on a bit of sleep.' We almost ran upstairs, like children who want to get upstairs and play, impatient to escape their parents.

'It's not a palace,' I warned Nedim, as we went into my bedroom and I closed the door behind us. I looked around us and my heart sank. It was worse than I'd imagined. The bed wasn't made, there were dirty clothes lying about, the window hadn't been opened for over a week and the air hung stale in the room to say the least. I'd had no idea when I walked out of this place that fateful day that I would be returning to it with a man I was in love with and wanted to impress. I felt horribly embarrassed. The place was a tip.

'My room's just the same as this,' Nedim said. 'I'm glad we came to yours first.'

I was grateful to hear him saying that. I said, 'Let's open the window for a minute, at least. And I'll do something with the dirty socks.'

As both our fathers had said to us, love will find a way. But we discovered then that love does something else: it makes allowances. Nedim said, quite matter-of-factly, 'Not just your socks.' He held up the bag he was carrying and that I'd temporarily forgotten about: the bag that contained the clothes we'd worn for a week and taken off in Trieste.

'There's a box on the landing,' I told Nedim. 'A woman collects the whole lot once a week.'

'Same where I live,' said Nedim, and as though it were the most normal thing to be doing, bent down and picked up my dirty socks, added them to the things in the bag, went out onto the landing and tipped the whole lot into the box. Then he came back in, closed the door again and gave me a real smacker of a kiss.

Nedim…

We were both discovering a phenomenal capacity for sleep. Falling together onto Braslav's bed – a single, but substantially wider than an Orient Express or Trieste *pensione* bunk – we were intending to have sex, of some sort, pretty much at once. We didn't. We woke up six hours later to find that we'd gone straight to sleep. We made up for the omission then, though; Braslav returning to me the compliment I'd paid him the last time we'd been to bed, in Trieste. Then, because we still had some money left over from the expenses the agent had given us, we went out to get something to eat.

We'd be going back to bed again shortly after dinner, we had agreed, because I had to get up in the morning at four o'clock, presumably leaving Braslav dozing between the sheets. We had to give a bit of thought to the question of when and where we would meet up next after that. It involved counting the coming days on our fingers as neither of us possessed any kind of diary or notebook.

Four days would elapse, we realised with dismay, before we could next meet up. Braslav would be returning from Trieste … with some other fireman, I couldn't help but reflect … early in the morning, shortly after I had set out on my shift on a saddle-tank. We agreed that Braslav would come and find me at the yard in the late afternoon, meeting me, as some of the wives sometimes met their husbands, as I came off shift. Then he would again take me back to his place.

Now, though, we were dining in a city-centre restaurant we'd only previously seen the outside of, on Viennese schnitzel with crushed potatoes, fried eggs and pickled cucumber salad.

'Nobody knows how the schnitzel came to be called Viennese,' Braslav said. 'It's originally a Croatian dish.'

I felt myself frown in puzzlement. 'I'd always heard it was originally Bosnian,' I said. This was the first thing we'd ever disagreed about. But if this was going to be the scale of our future disagreements … well, I thought we would probably be all right.

Braslav raised his glass of Mlava wine and said, *'Ziveli,'* which means live long or cheers.

I raised my own glass and said, *'Ziveli,'* back.

TWENTY

Nedim…

How shall I describe the emptiness of those three days? I was not brought up a Christian but I knew the story as well as anybody else. Those with my background are well acquainted with the story of the prophet Jesus. We have been told, we have read, how the world went dark when he expired on the cross, how the earth trembled and the Temple curtain broke. How he himself went to hell and back during the three days of his absence from earth…

I don't want to upset the sensibilities of readers who uphold the Christian faith, or to commit any act of blasphemy or disrespect, but I have to comment that Braslav's absence from me during those three days was a bit like that.

I went to work each day. I slept at night at my own apartment, not being bold enough to return to Braslav's in his absence and behave as if I owned the place. I cooked my poor suppers of stewed beans or scrambled eggs in the evenings. I didn't touch any alcohol. That was something that Braslav and I did together. Without him drinking made no sense. I didn't even masturbate. That was something else that we now did together. At least for three days I could let that wait. I found a map of the Orient Express routes at the office in the engine yard. I took it home with me and each evening I sat and pored over it. I peered, enchanted, at the names of the places we had visited together, and saw them in my mind, as we'd visited them by daylight or in the lamplit night: Vinkovci, Zagreb, Brod.

Then I'd look at the pinpoint that signified Trieste and try to imagine Braslav there now – which was difficult – and then at places farther afield: Sofia, Svilengrad and Istanbul to the south, Verona, Lausanne and Paris to the north. I didn't know if I'd ever get to see those places. Two weeks ago I'd scarcely dared to want to see them. Now I knew how much I did. I had dipped my toe in the water of travel since then. For the first time in my life I'd seen a bit of the world with Braslav. Now I wanted to see more of it.

All things must pass, as the old tale tells us. Including the three and a half days during which I had no contact with Braslav. I had one surreal experience during that time, though. The saddle-tank I was stoking passed 72619 in the Belgrade suburbs. She was being driven by a crew who knew nothing of our adventures and who didn't acknowledge me or the driver of my loco. It was like meeting a dog that you reared as a puppy but has now forgotten you since going to live with someone else. I wondered which engine Braslav had taken to Trieste this time. Was it another one he knew already? Was he attached to it?

The time did pass. I came into the shed at the end of my third day back at work on the saddle-tanks – I carried my night things with me in my knapsack in the hope that Braslav would be there and would take me home with him again as he had promised.

Life teaches you not to expect too much. I was braced for the possibility that, for whatever awful reason, Braslav would not turn up. But there he was, and my heart did a somersault in a rush of relief and love. That happened the moment I saw him. A second later, though, when we were walking towards each other, almost running in our excited haste, I saw there was something the matter. Braslav didn't look right.

Not caring about our many workmates bustling around us I tried to take him in my arms when we at last collided, but he shook me off. 'What's wrong?' I asked him, frightened now. He seemed somehow to be only half the size of his former self. There was a cut over his cheekbone and one eye was swollen and bloodshot. He looked as though someone had punched him in the face. 'What the fuck's happened to you?'

'Not here,' he said. 'We'll go to a café. Somewhere there are no ears.'

He turned and darted through a low brick archway into a small storage area where we kept the gas cylinders that were used for welding. From behind a stack of cylinders he reached out two battered suitcases. There was no need for him to tell me that they contained everything he owned in the world, including the dirty clothes that belonged to both of us. I had a vision of him fishing them distastefully out of the communal laundry box on the landing.

I skipped ahead two moves. 'You come and live with me,' I said.

He looked at me. 'You are lovely. I love you,' he said. A spill of tears ran suddenly down his face.

'I've got some iodine at home,' I said.

Over coffee Braslav told me all about it. He had returned from Trieste this morning and gone to his apartment to find two of the three men he shared it with sitting in the kitchen. They turned grim faces on him when he came in. 'We've had a meeting,' the one called Sergej had said. 'He can't live here. You can't have him staying here.'

'Why not?' Braslav had asked.

'He's not one of our people,' the other man had said.

'He's a Bosnian,' Braslav said. 'We're all Yugoslavian now. All Slavs. What difference does it make?'

'They're Muslim there,' Sergej said.

'And I'm a Catholic. From Croatia. I repeat: what difference does it make?'

'You're not one of us either,' said the other man. 'We've overlooked it till now. But this is Serbia here. Or it was till you lot came and pinched our jobs…'

'Pinched your jobs?!' said Braslav. 'We didn't. Look at you. You've all got jobs…'

'My brother hasn't,' objected Sergej.

'Look, this is ridiculous,' said Braslav, and he started to move towards the stairs.

'There's something else,' said Sergej. 'It's not just that. It's about you and that other bloke.' He stood up and so did the other man.

'What do you mean?' Braslav challenged him, though inside he was beginning to feel nervous.

'You know what we mean,' said the other man darkly. 'We don't need to spell it out. The meaning is that we want you out of here. Both of you. Muslim fancy-man and all.'

Braslav protested, argued with them for a few minutes. But during those minutes things got worse. The fourth member of the household arrived, coming home after a night shift, and pitched in on the side of the others against Braslav. They gave him an ultimatum. He could go and get his things – they'd give him ten minutes – and go peacefully. That or they would physically throw him out, minus belongings.

Against the three of them Braslav didn't stand a chance. Neither physically nor in reasoned argument. He went and packed his suitcases. When he came downstairs with them the others demanded he hand over his key to the apartment. Braslav had no choice. Then, while he was on his way to the door, one of them shoved him. Braslav turned and shoved him back. A brief, half-hearted scuffle broke out. Sergej half- threw a punch. It didn't hurt much or do much damage, Braslav said, but it had broken the skin on his cheek...

'And it caught your eye,' I said. 'We must take care of that.' I went on, 'What have you been doing all day?' Pathetically he told me that once he'd hidden his belongings in the gas hole he'd simply walked the streets. 'You should've gone to where I live,' I told him. 'They'd have taken you in. They're a hospitable people, my lot.'

Braslav smiled with rueful amusement. 'You've never given me your address.'

I said, 'Hell.' I wanted to kick myself. Then I thought – and then said, 'You never asked for it.' For the first time since we'd met this evening we both laughed.

We finished our coffees, then picked up the cases and walked to my apartment. I carried one of the cases, of course. Everybody knows this doesn't help a lot, as both of you have to walk off-balance and can end up pulling muscles in unexpected places. But everybody does this instinctively when they want to show solidarity and support, when they want to show friendship and love. The instinct is misguided. Perverse if you like. But it's wonderfully human. And very nice.

I'd thought wishfully a few days ago that Braslav would take care of me through thick and thin, look after me as his boy for the rest of our life. I realised now, growing up very suddenly in half an hour, that it wouldn't always be like that. Sometimes, as now, I would have to be the one who looked after Braslav, the one who made the decisions about what to do next. And I realised that this was how it should be. That what people were beginning to call "relationships" were better when they worked like that. Braslav would indeed look after me when he was able to. But I would look after him when he could not. A rush of emotion came over me as, weighed down awkwardly on one side only, we made our way through the slushy streets. I blurted, 'I want to look after you for ever, Braslav.'

'I'll look after you too,' he said quietly. 'Everything in my power.'

'We'll look after each other,' I said.

Braslav...

And so I moved in with Nedim, becoming his house guest for a period whose duration neither of us could guess. His place was as grubby and as poor as mine had been. I was perversely relieved by that.

His flat-mates were all young Bosnian Muslims who worked, as we did and as my ex-flat-mates did, on the railway. I'd seen them about the yard from time to time, though we'd never met. I'm ashamed to say that we Orient Express drivers – including me up to this time –

tended to hold ourselves a bit aloof. They – I mean Nedim's flat-mates – took to me readily, and welcomed me into their home. If they had suspicions about the nature of our friendship then they kept them hidden. If they were aware of our bedtime habits they seemed prepared to turn a blind eye to them.

A routine developed over the next week or so. We spent our evenings and nights together when I was in Belgrade, and Nedim had to make do with his own company while I was away on the Express, plying between Belgrade and Trieste. It was not a bad situation, although we missed each other painfully during our days apart. I kept reminding Nedim – and in reminding him reminded myself – that many pairs of lovers had periods of separation much longer and more difficult to face, but somehow that didn't seem to help.

During the times I spent by myself, walking by the docks in Trieste before bed sometimes, I tried to take stock of my situation and to think about what to do next. I had lost my old apartment, and felt myself well rid of those old flat-mates. Except that I wasn't entirely rid of them. Although our paths crossed rarely, they were still based at the yard, and I wondered if they were spreading tales about Nedim and me around the place. Occasionally I would get a look from some other railwayman that suggested my credibility as a 'normal' chap had taken a knock. Nobody said anything but... Or, more to the point, nobody had said anything *yet*.

Sometimes you have to be brave for the other person. Nedim had done this for me, inviting me to live with him, at the risk of alienating the people he lived with. Now it was my turn again.

I went to my foreman in his cubby-hole and told him I wanted Nedim promoted permanently to Orient Express fireman. Then I took a deep breath and added that I wanted Nedim to work alongside me on all my shifts. I wanted us to have identical schedules in other words. I was staking the whole of my reputation, a reputation I thought enhanced by my recent newspaper celebrity, on this. I finished my speech, stood and waited in front of the desk.

The foreman laughed in my face. 'Don't be ridiculous,' he said. 'If we could all get jobs for people we were hot for…' He laughed again as though this were the most entertaining moment of his day so far. It probably was. But for me it was rather the opposite. I had blown my cover, fired all my shots and had nothing to show for it. I walked away, shocked and dazed, and wondered what the impact of this disaster would be when news of it spread about the yard, as I knew it would. The repercussions would touch Nedim as well as myself. I told Nedim nothing about this for the moment, though I was afraid he would find out soon enough.

I walked around the city in a dizzy state, wondering what would happen and what I could possibly do next. Then the obvious struck me. I knew the name of the Compagnie director we had shared a carriage and a five-day adventure with. I knew the address of the

Compagnie's office in Paris. I wrote.

Cher Monsieur

I am the driver of the Orient Express train that was stuck in the snow two weeks ago near Brod, and on which you travelled. During that episode I had the honour to meet you once or twice.

I am now writing to ask your help in obtaining a favourable answer to an unusual but very special request.

You may have observed that a very strong bond grew between myself and the fireman who was with me on that journey, Nedim Osmanovic. However, we no longer have the opportunity to work together. I have tried without success to request promotion for Nedim to the status of full-time Orient Express fireman and also requested that we be allowed to work the same shifts.

Could you find it in your heart, mon cher monsieur, to persuade the supervisors at the locomotive yard in Belgrade to reconsider their decision on this matter?

I write in hope.

Your obedient servant

Braslav Horvat

I re-drafted the letter five times before I was a satisfied with it. Then, still without Nedim's knowledge, I posted it. I realised it might still get me nowhere. I had come as close as I dared to saying that Nedim and I were two men in love, and had thrown myself on the mercy of a near stranger, in the hope that he might be sympathetic to our circumstance. But venture nothing and you gain nothing. And the human heart can only live at all when it lives in hope.

TWENTY-ONE

Nedim…

I began to worry. Men who worked in the yard were giving me strange looks; at the same time Braslav seemed to worried by something. When I asked him about this he would withdraw and say, brusquely and unconvincingly, that nothing was worrying him at all. Then he'd at once say sorry, and he hadn't meant it to sound like that. I knew that he hadn't meant to sound brusque. He loved me and wanted everything in my life to be nice. That was the reason he was keeping something from me. He wanted to shield me from some unpleasantness. I was therefore obliged to try and guess what it was, and my guess was that somebody had said something or done something at the yard. At least there were no bruises on him. Every night we were together I looked very carefully for that.

Braslav…

A week passed and no letter came from Paris. I tried not to feel downcast, but I did. I tried not to let Nedim see that I felt that way, but he did. Then one morning my foreman came and found me soon after I'd brought an Express back from Trieste and was about to clock off. 'Surprise for you,' the foreman said. 'Your next run up to Trieste: you've got your fancy-man fireman with you again. Don't know how that came about. It was no doing of mine. And it's just a one-off exception to the normal routine. So don't get your hopes up for a repeat.'

I said, 'Don't call him my fancy-man. Nedim and I are friends. But thank you for telling me.' I walked away from him, and, although it wasn't quite the good news I'd been hoping for, I felt as though I was walking on air, simply because I had something to tell Nedim that would make him happy. I wondered if he would already have heard this news before I met him after his shift this afternoon. I wanted to be the one to tell him. I wanted to see his face light up. Nothing in my life before had ever made me as happy as the sight of Nedim's excited smile when I said something that he liked.

I came to the yard early and walked to the place where I knew his saddle-tank would dock. I waited for his arrival there, saw the little loco sidling across the points to its resting place for the night. There were still grey puddles between the tracks in the yard, but throughout the city and its outskirts most of the snow had cleared.

When the engine came to a stop its driver, who I knew slightly, peered down at me and greeted me in quite a friendly way, by name. 'I've a message for your fireman,' I said to him.

'Well, good,' the driver said. 'But for God's sake be careful, the two of you. You're getting yourselves talked about. I'm discreet. I'll say nothing about you walking over the tracks to meet him at the end of a shift, but others will notice. Just watch yourselves, that's all I say.'

That took some of the wind out of my sails, I must

admit, but still I was happy to see Nedim climb down to me a few seconds later, and I got a great kick out of giving him the news about our trip to Trieste the next day. I got a great kick out of his smile of joy too. 'Go and see your foreman,' I told him. 'Get it confirmed. I'd better not come with you though.' I jerked my head to where the other driver was now also climbing down from the cab and doing his best not to listen to us. 'I've had a friendly warning about being too obvious from your colleague here. I'll meet you at....' I named a café that was one of our regular haunts on our way home to Nedim's, and where the other railway workers didn't go.

Nedim...

That evening became a celebration. It began with a coffee in that café, but continued with beer – which I was just learning to get a taste for – then dinner with wine, then sex in bed. The enjoyment of everything was heightened by the knowledge that we would be working together for the next three days ... and it was sharpened still further by the fact of my not having to get up in the pre-dawn dark as I usually did, but being able to stay abed as long as I wanted to with Braslav: we didn't have to present ourselves in the yard till four o'clock the following afternoon.

When we did go to work, to prepare the loco and get steam up, I was braced and ready for ribald comments from the fellows in the yard, but none came, and we were left to ourselves as we worked, and even when we broke for coffee in the canteen. Another nice thing was the discovery that our engine was 72619. Braslav hadn't driven it since our adventure of three weeks ago. Braslav seemed as ready as I was to read a good omen into this.

When the time came to roll the engine backwards into the platform and down onto the waiting train there was another surprise for us. There was Sacha on the platform in the braid-decked uniform of *chef de train*. He'd been promoted. Braslav said, aside to me, that he hadn't seen him in the last few weeks, nor had he seen Andrea. It would be good to have a talk at some point, we told Sacha, if we got the chance between here and Trieste. For the moment we had to content ourselves with shaking hands.

And then we were off again into the dusk, gathering speed through the Belgrade suburbs and then hammering the rails along the valley of the Danube through the still thawing snow. It was an uneventful night. Vinkovci, Brod and Zagreb came and went. We climbed into the Alpine pass. The Italian border control guards checked our papers at Postojna as before. One of them actually smiled at me and chuckled. 'You were the one in the newspaper. I'd recognise that black face anywhere.' And then in the morning's early light we descended the looping track onto the Trieste spur.

But it was in Trieste that the big surprise came. Andrea brought the news of it. Actually, seeing him standing on the platform outside the cab was a surprise in itself. We hadn't had a chance to have a proper chat with Sacha during any of the stops, and we hadn't known till now that Andrea was on the train.

'You're not taking the southbound back to Belgrade,' Andrea told us once we'd shaken hands. 'They've got another crew for that. You're riding to Paris with us. All the way. As passengers, guests of the Compagnie...'

Braslav cut him off. 'You're joking...' But apparently Andrea was not. The Compagnie was planning a small ceremony in Paris the next day. An award would be given to each member of the crew of the train that had got stuck in the snow. They were all being recalled to Paris from wherever they were, their shifts covered by others as necessary...

The Compagnie agent was alongside us now. Was this true? we asked him. He said it was. But 72619 would still have to be driven away to the yard, Braslav pointed out. If we did that we'd miss...

'It's all been taken care of,' the agent said. 'A shunt crew are on their way. Just leave her here and catch your train before it goes...' And so we did.

Braslav...

We sat opposite each other at the window of a First-Class carriage on the Orient Express, in our own private compartment, enjoying the sight of Italy passing by outside. We weren't new to the experience of an Orient Express First-Class compartment of course. But being in one that was actually moving through sunlit scenery, rather than being iced up in a snowdrift, was something new to us. We didn't try to make passionate love on the carpet. We'd been doing that just eighteen hours ago and would be doing it again later, when the bunks were made up and it got dark. We were sharing a new discovery, Nedim and I: namely that living together with someone you love and fancy does begin to take some of the pressure off.

Instead we sat with lower legs intertwined by way of physical contact, and enjoyed the simple but novel pleasure of watching Italy rolling past. We hugged the coast at first, then the coast left us and we followed an inland route till we met the sea again at Venice. Venice! We had just a tantalising glimpse of it. We leaned from the window as we crossed the sea-bridge, wishing perversely that we could swap our carriage-window view of the approach for the one enjoyed in far less comfort by the Italian footplatemen through their forward cab lookout. We got out onto the platform at the terminus, and had just time to wander outside the building and see the Grand Canal, with waterbuses and gondolas bobbing on it, and lined with mansions of fairytale design, while the engine was unhitched and a fresh one reversed down to pull us out again.

Verona sparkled in the afternoon sun and a short time later so did the blue waters of Lake Garda. Then we dived into mountain valleys and threaded our way to Milano.

We'd had lunch in the restaurant car – two roughly dressed but otherwise inconspicuous passengers – and later we had dinner there as well. Was Roman the chef on this trip? Braslav asked our waiter. No, he wasn't, the waiter told us. He would be at the ceremony tomorrow, though. As evening came on we threaded our way between the beautiful Italian lakes. We changed direction, and because of that, changed engines, several times in Italy. At Venice, at Milan, and then as we approached Switzerland, at Domodossola. To my surprise Nedim had brought a map with him. We followed our route on that, until we plunged into the Simplon tunnel, which took us under the border between Italy and Switzerland. By the time we emerged from it onto the high, winding route through Switzerland dinner was finished, our wine was drunk, our bunks had been made up...

We didn't wake until we were on the approach to Paris.

Nedim...

I had moved into a new place. Not just physically. Not just into Paris by way of Venice and Milan ... and Lausanne and Dijon while I slept. I had moved into a different place inside myself. I don't know how to put this in a better way, how to write something more "sophisticated".

We were all put up at the grand hotel that is part of the Gare de Lyon terminus. We found our rooms, had a mid-morning cuddle on the beautifully quilted bed, then changed into fresh clothes – thank God we'd both thought to bring a set – before heading downstairs and into the hall of the restaurant that is named after the *Train Bleu.* This was the grandest space I'd entered in my life. A sky-blue ceiling over-arched us, supported by hoop-like gilded plaster vaults. White-clothed tables took the floor like dancers. It was like the restaurant car in the Orient Express, but ten times as magnificent and twenty times as big.

There were drinks first. A new drink had just been invented – by a man in Dijon, I was told, who was incredibly a Catholic priest. It consisted of white wine from that region – Burgundy – and some blackcurrant liqueur. What can I say about it? Like every alcoholic drink I'd tasted in the last month it tasted wonderful and somehow perfect. But I was learning from experience. I only had one glass of it. I knew there would be wine with lunch.

There was. There was champagne and burgundy, and Gigondas from the Rhone, and Châteauneuf du Pape. We ate eggs that were set like jewels in Aspic, then smoked trout, then a stew of chicken in red wine. There was cheese, and a feather-light fruit tart.

Then came speeches. The president of the Compagnie made one of them. Another was made by a Compagnie director I recognised. He was the one who'd shared the Athens-Paris coach with us a month before. Actually less than a month. A month, a little month… Yet so much had happened in the meantime that it now seemed long ago. I remembered it almost as one remembers a dream. The fact that it was a reality was only brought home to me by the presence of Braslav in my bed when I woke up on two or three mornings every week – and by the continuing numbness, caused by the mild frostbite I'd suffered then, of the littlest toes on my feet.

High-ranking representatives of the press were at that lunch. They took our photographs. No, this time I didn't show them a blackened face. Then we stood, we lined up – all those of us who had served the Compagnie during those testing, eventful days – Roman had joined us by now, and there were Sacha and Andrea along with all the rest – and received a medal each (pinned to our chests by the president of the Compagnie, no less) and then an envelope. None of us was so ill-bred as to open his envelope in public and in the glare of the camera flashes of Europe's press.

Then we sat down again, not necessarily in the same seats we'd sat in while we ate our lunch, and were served coffee and Cognac. Roman joined us for a few minutes. He was friendly but no more than that. The closeness that had sprung up between all of us during that first day's reconnaissance trip in the snow had not lasted. I remembered the moment when we had all hugged one another, in tears with the emotion of returning safely to the temporary homeliness and warmth of our marooned Express. How, a couple of hours later, Braslav had gone into the restaurant-car kitchen to take Roman's boots off and rub his frost-bitten feet back to life. How Roman had agreed most willingly to spending not just one night but two on Sacha's divan in the corridor so that Sacha and Andrea could spend time together in the privacy of a berth. That was big of Roman, I had to give him that.

But I couldn't help remembering also how unpleasantly he had crowed when the mere accidents of his having a gun with him and Braslav's being attacked by a wolf had wrung the leadership of our party from Braslav's grasp and laid it within reach of his. Yet later Braslav and he seemed to have patched things up: they had paid generous tributes to each other at the Trieste press conference. Perhaps Roman simply had mixed feelings about homosexual relationships, I thought, as after a few minutes with us he got up, politely bade us au revoir and moved away to join a group with whom he felt more comfortable. That was reasonable enough, I told myself. If I was going to go through life with Braslav beside me I might have to get used to quite a lot of that. It was better than outright hostility at least.

I was surprised, a few minutes later, to see the Compagnie director who had shared our carriage with us heading towards our table with a look on his face that indicated he was coming to join us. I suddenly remembered that he'd seen me naked in the corridor once when I'd darted out of our compartment to pick up a tray of food and drink. I flushed hot and cold at the memory. Was he coming over to remonstrate with me about that?

When he reached our table he bowed slightly and, smiling in turn at both Braslav and myself, asked if we would allow him to join us. It seemed slightly less likely now that he was coming to give me a ticking-off, and a cautious wave of relief came over me as, following our quick assent, he sat down beside us. The next thing he did surprised me somewhat. He took a small cigar case out of his pocket and offered a cigar to me and one to

Braslav – we both accepted – and then he lit all three of them with a silver lighter which had his initials engraved on it.

He gave me another quick smile as I drew on the first cigar of my life and tried to look as though I knew what I was doing with it. Then, to my further surprise on this trip of surprises, he addressed Braslav. 'I owe you an apology, Monsieur,' he said. 'I have not replied to your letter yet. You already know that, I think.' He chuckled. 'However, it is not the case that I have taken no action on your behalf. Unfortunately, though, I have met with no success.'

I was astonished to hear this. Braslav had been in correspondence with this high-ranking official? I was agog to know what this might be about. I didn't interrupt, though. I guessed that if I sat and listened patiently I would in due course find out.

'I did ask our Belgrade agent to speak directly with your superiors at the railway depot. I'm afraid the answer he got was not the most polite. So, I am sorry to have to say that, although I've had your best interests at heart and have tried to assist you in your quest, I have come a cropper, as the English say, at the first fence.'

I could see the look of disappointment on Braslav's face, though I still had no idea what all this could be about. But Braslav said stoically, 'I can only thank you for trying, Monsieur. I thank you most humbly, from the bottom of my heart.' Sometimes I felt that Braslav rather overdid the humble bit. One day I might tell him about this. If our relationship survived long enough. And if I felt brave enough.

But the director hadn't finished yet. He held his hand up to show that he had more to say, puffed on his cigar once and said, 'I do not want my efforts to help you to be remembered as a failure. Not by you both,' he acknowledged me with a quick smile and a nod, 'nor by myself. So, with some misgiving, because you may not like or want it, I have a different proposal to make. Feel free to dismiss my offer out of hand if you wish to, but I hope you will hear me out first.'

The man was going to make some sort of proposal? To both of us? Whatever had been going on between him and Braslav behind my back? But there was no question of my refusing to listen to whatever he might say next. And the same clearly went for Braslav, since at the same moment we both nodded our vigorous assent. Braslav, his face now all expectation, took a manly pull on his cigar. I looked at mine, saw it had not actually gone out yet, and decided that my next manly puff could wait.

TWENTY-TWO

Braslav...

The Compagnie Internationale des Wagons-Lits did not employ the drivers and firemen who crewed its trains. It employed the on-board catering and passenger-management staff. Roman, Sacha and Andrea, for example, were Compagnie staff. Nedim and I were not. Drivers and firemen, and the engines they piloted, were hired by the Compagnie from the railway infrastructure companies of the various countries the train passed through. The contracts required that a loco, a driver and a fireman were provided at each country border: that was all. I've probably explained this already. Sorry if I have, but in repeating it now I want to make the point that Monsieur Bouc, the Compagnie director, was neither my boss, nor my boss's boss, nor my boss's boss's boss. He was simply a client, if you like, or a partner, of the Yugoslavian state railway, for whom Nedim and I worked. That is why it was a rather big thing – a rather cheeky or a rather desperate thing – for me to have written to him in the first place.

And that is why I was astonished to hear M. Bouc say suddenly, 'I should like to offer you both a job.'

Nedim...

You could have knocked me down with a rolled-up pancake. Jobs for both of us? But I wondered, what sort of jobs? Washing plates and stacking dishes in the kitchen of the Orient Express?

I heard the Compagnie director say smoothly, as if seamlessly following my thoughts, 'And I don't mean stacking dishes or washing plates. The Compagnie operates several Orient Express services out of Paris. One you have just travelled on. Another runs quite separately, from the Gare du Nord to Calais, where it meets the English packet boat. Two more run from the Gare de l'Est towards Germany and Austria...' He stopped and smiled self-deprecatingly for a moment. 'Gentlemen, of course you know all this. I mention it only to remind you of the sheer size and complexity of the Compagnie's operations. To run all these services we depend on the French railway network to supply the drivers and firemen. Just as we have depended on the Yugoslavian railway to supply you and others to drive our trains between Belgrade and Trieste.'

He paused another moment. He pulled on his cigar. So did Braslav. And, for better or worse, I also did.

'Sometimes the system lets us down,' the director said. 'There are miscommunications – these things happen – or personnel go sick. Unavoidable in any large organisation, but as a result trains sometimes run late. So we are thinking of putting a driver and a fireman on our own payroll, to cover eventualities such as these. In addition to covering the French sections of all those routes the two new staff might find themselves being ferried as far afield as Turkey to pick up a train, or to drive from Germany to Austria and back. The men we choose for this purpose will of necessity be based in

Paris. In the absence of any emergencies such as those I have hypothesised, they will not be sitting on their … um … seats, but will be found plenty of other work. The pay will be appropriate to the responsibility involved, and the men to whom we offer these positions, driver and fireman, will certainly earn it… Messieurs, I would like to offer the two of you this opportunity. If you are at all interested we can talk further. If not, please stop me at this point and we can finish our cigars in a friendly way over a final brandy.'

Braslav…

We didn't stop M. Bouc. We were interested. We did talk further. And we had another brandy.

Nedim…

The afternoon seemed to float. The four of us – Sacha and Andrea, Braslav and I – walked in the early spring sunshine. Leaving the Gare de Lyon we found ourselves on the quays of the Seine within seconds. A few more minutes and we were looking across the water at the elegant façades of the mansions on the Ile de St Louis. We crossed a bridge a little later and found ourselves on the Ile de la Cité, viewing the sturdy towers and needle-like spire of the cathedral of Notre Dame. We went inside. It was my first step inside a Christian church. It would take too long to explore the complex feelings this gave me. I'll make do with saying that that experience – stepping into a realm of quiet echoes and light that had filtered through vast windows of red and blue glass – was one of great beauty and one that I will never forget.

Then we crossed back to the Ile de St Louis by a small footbridge and sat there in the sun outside the ice-cream parlour Chez Berthillon, drinking coffee and eating ice-cream while the waters of the Seine met bubbling around the eastern point of the City Island just thirty yards away, only to separate again as they encountered the west tip of St Louis Island just below the promenade on which we sat.

'How do you manage it?' Braslav asked the other two. 'I mean, keeping your relationship hidden – staying together for each other when you must have different timetables sometimes, different shifts…'

'Our salvation,' Sacha answered, 'is Paris. As yours will be. We have a small apartment in the eighteenth arrondissement, on the poorer side of Montmartre. But it is heaven for us.'

'And your neighbours think…?'

'There is no law outlawing homosexual acts in France,' said Sacha. 'Although there is plenty of disapproval from religious people…'

Andrea interrupted with a giggle. 'And from some others who are absolutely not religious!' He shovelled a dainty piece of ice-cream into his mouth.

Sacha smiled at him but went on smoothly, 'Sometimes we deliberately let people misunderstand the situation: we let them suppose we are brothers.'

'How do you manage that?' I asked naively.

'We lie baldly to them,' said Andrea. It seemed to make sense.

We talked throughout the afternoon and evening, enjoying a small supper all together in our hotel. Sacha and Andrea might have an apartment just a couple of miles away but they were not going to miss out on a night in a grand hotel, paid for by the Compagnie. After supper we continued to linger in the ornately decorated, high-ceilinged bar, each sipping one final Cognac. The others also had a last cigar of the evening, but I decided to decline the offer of that. By the time we parted company for the night in the richly carpeted corridor between our two bedrooms it had been agreed that when we arrived in Paris to start work a month from now Sacha and Andrea would put us up in their apartment for a period while they helped us to find a place of our own. It would mean sleeping on a floor or a sofa for a bit, but we had no objection at all to that.

For tonight though… We had our first experience of a night in a grand hotel. A room that was four times as big as a Wagon-Lit compartment. A wash-basin with a design of birds and flowers upon its shiny concave surface. An art-nouveau armoire in mahogany that was so big that we felt almost ashamed that we had only one coat apiece to hang in it. A chest of drawers to match. A chandelier hung from the ceiling, sparkling and spangling overhead. But more wonderful than all these luxurious modern marvels was something else: our first experience of sharing a double bed.

Braslav…

The following morning Sacha and Andrea were our tour guides around Paris. They showed us the Eiffel Tower – fifty years old this year, Sacha told us proudly, as if he himself had built it – and the enormous Arc de Triomphe. We travelled on another western wonder – the underground railway that was Paris's Métro, and I wondered when if ever Belgrade might have something like it running beneath its streets.

In the evening, after our day of sightseeing, our recent journeys – we had been on more than a merely geographical one – went into reverse. We spent the next night and day as passengers on the Orient Express as the Compagnie's honoured and decorated guests, arriving at evening in the coastal warmth of Trieste. Then we returned to our roles as driver and fireman, employees of the Yugoslavian railway company, for the long leg home to Belgrade.

Home… Hmmm. The good news was that Belgrade would remain our home for only one more month while we worked our notice out. At the end of that period we would be transferring ourselves, lock stock and barrel, to Paris. We could hardly wait.

Nedim…

How strange that transition time was: the month in which we worked our notice. In a sense things had returned to the way they had been before. I spent my days on the saddle-tanks, shuttling to and fro along the suburban lines around Belgrade. Braslav continued to be away for days at a time, taking the Orient Express to Trieste and back. (And I continued to envy him that!) When he was in Belgrade he continued to live at my apartment and share my small bed.

But in another sense everything had changed completely. We stood at the gateway to a new life. A life in a city where two men could live together fairly openly. (Although Sacha had warned us that even in Paris we wouldn't be able to have sex in the street. We had laughed and said that, since we were going to be sharing a flat together we would hardly need to be doing that.)

We were looking at a future together, Braslav and I. Living together and working in harness. Living in the most beautiful capital city of Europe: a place where both men and women were elegant, sophisticated and beautifully dressed; a city whose food and drink were unsurpassed...

Don't get carried away, Braslav would warn me during those weeks. No place on earth is perfect, he would say. Sacha had told him that in winter Paris could be as cold and dismal as anywhere else on earth. 'I know,' I would tell him. 'I'm not a child. I do understand things like that. Paris is quite far north. But sometimes getting carried away is nice.'

Less nice was the atmosphere at work. Not that anything happened to us. Neither of us got beaten up or even shouted at. But the looks we got on our return from

Paris… If looks could kill… Fortunately they can't.

A fellow came up to me one morning, though, while I was filling my wheelbarrow with kindling in the early morning dark. 'Is it true, what they say about you?' he asked.

'No idea,' I answered, continuing to pull split lengths of old sleepers from the stack. 'What do they say about me?'

'That you're a fairy queen or whatever they call it. That you and that nose-in-the-air little driver who works on the…'

'Call us what you like,' I said. 'Names can't hurt.' I let my armful of kindling fall into the barrow with a rumble of thwacks and turned to face him square. He turned and walked away with a snort. Walked away rather quickly, I thought. Normally I was not a confrontational person. I had a timid streak running through me, to tell the truth, and normally shrank from scenes like that. However sometimes you just have to stand up for yourself and those you love. And when those situations arose for me … well, it did help that I was built like the proverbial brick shit-house.

It remained that way at work throughout those last few weeks. The drivers I worked with and the firemen Braslav worked with remained civil to us, though I thought sometimes, only just. But in the mess canteen hardly anyone would speak to us. It hurt a little but not too much. I had my Braslav and he had me. Together we had *us*.

We spent our free time alone together, sitting at cafés in the lengthening spring evenings, sleeping in my apartment at night. I have to say in fairness that we never had trouble with the other fellows at my apartment. They may not have consorted with us at the yard, but at home they remained pleasant enough.

A thought struck me one of those evenings with Braslav. We were sitting at a pavement table outside one of our regular café haunts. He'd been telling me stories about his childhood among the mountains a little way inland from Split. 'What was your father's name?' I asked.

'Kristian,' he answered at once. That seemed fairly conclusive. I said no more on the subject.

TWENTY-THREE

Nedim…

I don't know whether it was a sign of our old employers wanting to wring the last drop out of us, or an act of generosity on their part, or a mixture of the two – something I later heard defined as enlightened self-interest. But whatever their motives were, we found ourselves doing our last ever shift for the Yugoslavian railway company together, on the Orient Express, doing the overnight run from Belgrade to Trieste. We had our final pay packets with us. 'You're being paid your final shift in advance,' said Jusuf as he handed me mine. Don't abscond at Vinkovci.' He was only half joking, I could see. 'Why would I do that?' I asked him. 'When I'm on my way to Paris.'

'You're just a big girl, Nedim,' he said. He took the pencil from behind his ear, twirled it once in his fingers, then put it back in its accustomed place. Then he walked away with a snort.

The snow was all gone now. As we drove through the night the sleepers showed dark between the silver rails in the light of our headlamp and the fields lay black, no longer bluish white, to either side of us. But when dawn broke as we headed down towards Italy from the Alpine heights I saw that the slopes were carpeted with blue flowers. The sight was … here comes a word I have only used once before in this narrative … glorious. I was reminded of the blue and silver patterned bedspread that had covered our large bed in the hotel on the Gare de Lyon. 'You didn't tell me about this, Braslav,' I complained to him. He'd been here much more recently, and much more often, than I had.

'Didn't I?' He answered. 'I meant to, I think, but I forgot.'

'A bridge you forgot to cross when you came to it,' I said. He laughed at that and, reaching across the cab, gave me a kiss. And then, between the mountains, the sea came shining round a corner at us and Braslav closed the regulator as we coasted the looping route down to Trieste.

From Trieste we rode as passengers, as the Compagnie's guests, traversing Italy during the afternoon and Switzerland and France that night. Neither Sacha nor Andrea was working that particular shift. They met us at the Gare de Lyon, though: they were waiting at the barrier for us as we disembarked that morning and lugged our suitcases up the platform; they shepherded us onto a bus that took a route I was sure I would never remember, through the centre of Paris and up the steep hill to Montmartre and to their flat.

It was a small and simple apartment, of course; we'd expected nothing else. But it had something very special about it. Its windows had a view down the eastern slopes of Montmartre and all across Paris. Sacha pointed out to us the Opéra, the Panthéon, the Gare du Nord and the Gard de l'Est, and the wooded hillside of the Bois de Vincennes where, he said, the Paris zoo was. Then he and Andrea took us back downstairs again and out into the sunshine. We walked no more than five paces from our new front door before we arrived at a line of café tables and chairs on the pavement, sat down, and had a coffee there. We were still on our new home turf: the front windows of Sacha and Andrea's apartment looked down on us from directly above. While we were there we were introduced to the patron of the café and his wife. I think I understood from Sacha's French that he had introduced us as another pair of brothers... I remembered what he'd told us about that. I felt suddenly happy. I thought we'd made a brilliant start.

Braslav...

So began a routine that was as perfect as any routine can be that involves the need to get up and go to work. Our social lives became enmeshed with Sacha's and Andrea's. Though in a good way. They were often absent for days at a time, and so were we, and those days didn't always coincide. Our paths crossed often, but not so often that we got under each other's feet at the apartment.

Within a month, though, we had found an apartment of our own, with Sacha's and Andrea's help. It was in the Rue La Barre, just two blocks away from where they lived in the Rue Nicolet. It was airy and high up and, like their apartment, had views across eastern Paris. It comprised a small sitting room, a neat kitchen with a seating area that had a fixed table and bench seats, and there was a bathroom and a toilet. What's more, the bedroom was furnished with a double bed. We made the most of that.

Our work... That too was good. We worked out of Paris often. Sometimes we headed north to Calais, and were astonished the first time we went there in good weather to see a line of chalk cliffs across the water. We were told it was England we were looking at. 'One day we'll go there,' Nedim said.

'England, gateway to America,' I said jokingly.

But Nedim gave me a solemn look. 'We'll go there too,' he said.

We drove the French section of our old Simplon Express route. That took us past Dijon and Dole to just short of the Swiss border, to a little place called Vallorbe, where we would turn the engine and then head back to Paris. And we drove the other Orient routes, one to Châlons, Nancy and Strasbourg, the other towards Basel via Belfort.

More rarely we covered other drivers and firemen who were on leave of absence in other countries. We got to drive – if only occasionally – in Italy, Germany, Yugoslavia(!), Bulgaria and Thrace. We never found ourselves on the Swiss section of the Simplon route. We never learned the reason for this, but as the years passed we began to make a joke of it. The Swiss, we told each other, were simply never, ever, late for work

But the best thing of all, better than the globe-trotting aspect of it, was that nearly always we were together on the same footplate.

Quite often though, to return to our first months in Paris, there was no driving or stoking work on a particular day, for either of us. M. Bouc had told us that on those days work would be found for us. But we had been taken a little by surprise when he told us that momentous afternoon in the *Train Bleu* restaurant about the nature of that work.

We joined the staff of the archive of the Compagnie, cataloguing old press cuttings among other things and filing new ones. The chief of this department, a white-haired man with a scholarly temperament, was French. He spoke a little German and a little English. We came to understand that we were considered a bit of a find by the Compagnie: we spoke and read German fluently and also Serbo-Croat. We could make sense of some of the more obscure archive material that others could not. I've made it sound as though the archive department was run by a massive staff. It wasn't of course. Everyone who worked there did it on a part-time basis. They – we – all did other jobs within the Compagnie. It was a fascinating new experience for us both. We learned so much about the extraordinary history of the Compagnie Internationale des Wagons-Lits. And little by little, as time passed, we learnt to speak and read French.

I already knew that Nedim had read a little Goethe and Shakespeare. Now, as we worked together in the archive, I began to see that for someone of his background he was surprisingly well-educated. At least in the sense that he had learnt things from newspapers and books. The same went for me too actually. Eventually I had to ask.

I chose a moment when we were lying in bed together one evening in the midsummer of that first year in Paris. Outside it was still light. 'Nedim,' I began, 'tell me what your father was like.'

His father had disappeared, I already knew, when Nedim was eight. But up to that time, Nedim remembered, he had thought of him as gentle, kind and good. He it was who had taught him to read, Nedim told me now. He had taken him to their local town of Travnik and shown him there the public reading room where grave be-whiskered men sat pondering books and newspapers in a fug of cigar and cigarette smoke. His father had urged him to make use of that facility when he grew older, in the cause of "bettering" himself.

It all sounded terribly familiar. How well I remembered the public reading room in Split.

'Of course I didn't get very far with my book learning,' Nedim prattled on. 'I stayed a fireman, Still am one. It wasn't till the day I met you that I really "bettered myself". He chuckled at his own joke and wriggled one hand round behind my neck; with the other he lightly tickled my cock.

'That's very sweet,' I said, and kissed him. 'And it goes for me too. And it goes without saying that the day

I met you – it was the same day you met me of course –
was the day I "bettered myself" too.'

But I wanted to keep the conversation serious.
'Nedim,' I asked him, 'what did your father look like?'

'Oh,' he said, and sounded dismayed. He withdrew
his hand from my cock, though he left the other one
round my neck and now he stroked me reassuringly with
it. I knew then that he knew where I was leading him. He
said, 'I didn't know you'd been thinking about that.'

'I'm sorry,' I said. 'I didn't know you'd been thinking
about it.'

Then haltingly, bit by bit, during the next hour as we
lay in bed, it all came out. We had the conversation we'd
been putting off for months but had separately known
we would one day have to have.

We described our fathers' forearms and their lips.
Their noses and the gaps among their teeth. The way
they laughed, they way they smiled… The way they
spoke, the things they said.

The way he spoke. The things he said.

We counted our early years on our fingers beneath the
sheets. There remained a few years during our
childhoods during which we couldn't account for him.
'Perhaps he was also a Serbian Orthodox,' suggested
Nedim, 'or a Hassidic Jew. Or both.'

'A Swiss Calvinist?' I offered, and then to my great

relief we found we were both able to laugh a bit, although not very heartily, at the absurdity of all this. I said, 'I don't know if I feel nice about this or if...'

'I know,' said Nedim. 'You don't need to say it.'

I said, 'It's still not midnight. Let's put our clothes back on, go out and find a bar and have a drink.'

'Best idea I've heard yet,' said Nedim, stepping with astonishing alacrity out of the warm bed.

We sat out late on the pavement, drinking Cognac. It seemed an appropriate drink.

We tried to guess what our father had really been like. We both knew him as a travelling salesman by trade, so that was something solid we could both cling on to: he hadn't told different stories about that at least. But where had he got his book learning? What was he doing in those missing years when he lived neither with Nedim and his mother nor with me and mine? We had no idea. In the end we could only speculate and wildly guess. Unless he were to show up one day... We thought this unlikely. We would have to live with the mystery unsolved. But after all, we told each other, wasn't that a common enough case with families of all sorts? It was Nedim who finished by quoting the saying: 'It's a wise child that knows his own father.' He was right. I told him that, and put my hand over his – rather boldly, rather publicly – between the balloon glasses on the table top.

That was nice. We had done the easy bit. But now we

couldn't avoid the nub of the matter. We had to deal with it. I took a deep breath. 'It's the sex thing, isn't it?' I said to Nedim. He nodded and murmured yes.

It was fortunate perhaps that I'd already had a couple of months to ponder this. Just in case the suspicions I'd had were to be confirmed – as now tonight they had been. I gave Nedim the benefit of my months'-worth of thoughts. He could take them or leave them as he considered fit.

'Incest is prohibited in most societies,' I said. 'And has been through most of history. We both know that. But think about the reason for this.'

Nedim startled me by coming in straight away. 'It's biology,' he said. 'What they call genetics.'

'My God, you've been thinking about this too.' I said.

He said, 'You bet I have.'

'Well, what's the genetic thing about, then?' I answered myself. 'Things can go wrong when close blood relations produce children together. That's what it's about. That's all it is. That's what the taboo, the stigma, the laws and all the moral objections – the question of sin and so forth – are all about.'

Nedim looked across the table directly into my face. 'You're saying, are you, that because we aren't remotely capable of producing children together the taboo should not apply to us?' He held my gaze very sternly for a moment and, although with some difficulty, I held his.

'Yes,' I said. 'I think that is what I'm saying. Yes,' I couldn't read the expression in his face. 'Listen, Nedim,' I went on gently. 'Do you still love me?' He breathed a yes. 'Do you still find me attractive?' He nodded, and I suddenly felt his hand alight on my knee beneath the table-top. God, what a wonderful feeling that was just then! How much it meant! 'Do you still want to sleep with me tonight?'

'I do,' he said, and there was a sudden renewal of strength in his voice. 'I want that, and I want you, more than anything else on earth.'

'It's the same for me,' I said. 'So why don't we do just that? Then take it from there.'

And that is what we did.

TWENTY-FOUR

Nedim…

We took it from there that night. We finished our Cognacs and walked home. On the short way back from the Place de Tertre where we'd had our drink, round the back of the Sacré Coeur Basilica, I felt Braslav bravely take my hand in his. And so, for the first time ever, we walked a little way through the streets of Paris hands clasped. It was Braslav's doing, that. I'd never felt more proud of him. I'd never loved him more than I did tonight.

How often have I written that! But it has been the truth every time.

We went back to bed. No, the trauma of our just ended discussion had not dampened our physical passion for each other. If anything the reverse was the case. I caressed my lover's warm skin with my hands, enjoying the contrast between the smooth and the hirsute bits. Then Braslav rolled me gently sideways and entered me from behind, one arm protectively around my shoulder. We rocked to and fro together, as if imagining the gentle swaying of an Express carriage in the night. Braslav climaxed quietly and thoughtfully inside me. Then, a few minutes later, we rolled round till we lay the other way, me behind him. Then, in my turn, I slid myself inside Braslav. I'd learnt to do this without hurting him by now. It was very nice. Especially tonight. Making love is the polite expression for having sex. I wasn't sure if sex could actually create love. But (if I hadn't realised it already, then this night I would have done) having sex can certainly reinforce it.

In the morning as we lay in bed for a few minutes before getting up I was struck by a thought that made me giggle. I sat up and told Braslav. 'My father was circumcised, like every practising Muslim. Did you – not to mention your mother – never notice that?'

'There are things you have yet to learn,' Braslav said. 'Circumcision isn't unheard of among Catholics.' He paused then and I could almost hear him thinking back to old sexual encounters. 'And even, I believe,' he finished, 'among Protestants.' He sat up and glanced at his watch, where it hung as usual on the wall beside the bed. 'Time for up, big boy,' he said, and pulled the blankets back. 'Can't have us late for work.'

Braslav...

We took it from there in the months that followed. As far as our blood relationship went we were actually only half-brothers, of course. But as lovers we made up for that. Nedim was a lover and a half. He was kind enough to say the same of me.

Two years passed in blissful happiness. Then another incident befell the Orient Express, and we were involved in it. A train on the Vienna-Budapest branch of the Express's route was blown up in September 1931. A Hungarian bomber, thought at the time to be a Fascist, then later a Communist, detonated a bomb beneath the Biatorbagy Bridge near Budapest as the train approached. Unable to stop, the engine ploughed ninety feet down the river bank, dragging nine of the train's eleven carriages after it. Twenty-three people died and many more were injured.

We didn't learn all the dreadful details at once. We were simply called out of bed in the middle of that September night and ordered to take fresh rolling stock out to the scene of the disaster, to bring the passengers back to Paris. We didn't drive all the way, of course. We handed the train over to a Swiss crew at Basel and waited there a day and a half for it to come back. Thus does one man's catastrophe make a day's holiday for someone else. Only later, on the drive back did we begin to hear the rumours of the cause of the crash. It was the Fascists. It was the Communists. We could take our pick.

Fascists, Communists. The world east of Paris was beginning to look a dangerous place. The man who was King of Yugoslavia, the Serbian Alexander I, was shot and killed by Fascists in Marseilles in 1934. He had been on his way to Paris for a state visit, seeking support for his country and treaty links with democratic France. He was succeeded by an eleven-year-old…

Nedim and I talked sometimes about going back. But back to what? We had no families in Yugoslavia and no particular friends there. As men who loved each other we would have been more conspicuous in Belgrade's streets than we were in Paris. The new man in Germany,

Adolph Hitler, appeared to be fishing for friends in Yugoslavia, with a view to carving it up one day with Benito Mussolini, his Italian friend... At least, the papers said that.

We didn't go back. Was that unpatriotic of us? Perhaps it was. But we thought of ourselves as French now. We had our lives here, we had our home, we had our jobs.

We were promoted. We didn't stop driving trains but we had the additional responsibility of liaising with German- and Serbo-Croat-speaking national railway networks when difficulties arose that concerned locomotives or footplate crews. We became accustomed to using the telephone. Had our first tastes of office work. Less enjoyable than the footplate, at least in summer, but we were glad of the rise in pay. We moved into a slightly larger apartment, just one block nearer the summit of Montmartre, in the Rue Lamarck.

Nedim...

We took it from there in the years that followed too. That momentous conversation, the one in which we admitted our blood relationship, occurred on a September night. And it seemed that all the big things that followed happened in September too. September 1931 was the Budapest disaster. September 1938 saw Hitler's annexation of the part of Czechoslovakia called the Sudetenland.

Two of the Orient Express's routes ran past the

Sudetenland, one on either side. The writing seemed to be on the wall for the Express's routes in Eastern Europe. Who knew what would happen when fighting broke out along the line? Who knew what would happen if fighting broke out nearer home? For it would come. We knew that now. But where? In the streets of Belgrade? In Paris? Surely not. Yet when it came –we had to ask ourselves – whose side would we be on? Come to that, whose side would anybody be on?

Nedim... 26th August 1939

Today Croatia became an autonomous state. For the first time since the Great War. Though it was hardly autonomous back then, as Braslav reminded me. It was part of the Habsburgs' giant territory: the Austro-Hungarian Empire.

'And it's hardly going to be autonomous now,' Braslav said, jabbing with a finger at the newspaper in which we'd read the news. 'Its independence guaranteed and underwritten by Mussolini and Hitler, for pity's sake!' He made a face of disgust. We were glad we hadn't gone back.

'Boys, boys...' Sacha was calling us to heel. And we came willingly. It was his birthday, and we were celebrating the occasion with him and Andrea at their apartment in the Rue Nicolet, drinking their champagne. On everybody's birthday tragic events occur somewhere in the world; they give no-one an excuse not to celebrate the occasion. No-one who isn't involved in the tragedy directly, that is.

We have become very close to Sacha and Andrea as the years have passed. They are the only people we have ever shared our big secret with. Except occasionally in an odd sort of way, when people have expressed surprise at two men sharing an apartment together and we, following Sacha's initial advice, have said, 'Oh, we're brothers.' And that has been that. We've been telling the truth when we've said that – we were telling the truth even before we knew it was the truth in fact – and the only lie has been one of omission. We haven't gone on to say that we sleep together in a carnal way, or that even after knowing each other for ten years we remain in deepest love.

Sometimes you can go too far when telling the truth, and so we don't attempt to. That's something that our father obviously knew about.

Ten years we've been together. Ten years we've been unremittingly in love. And the years have treated us not too badly. We still enjoy our work together, our travel, and our good health and looks.

Looking outside, looking east, the situation frightens us. But what can we really do? Join the Communists? They don't have the guns that Hitler has, or that Mussolini has. Our old comrade Roman would be the first to tell us that. It's only when we look inwards that we find comfort, truth be told. Our friendship with Sacha and Andrea sustains us too, I think now. We are talking, over our champagne, about the extraordinary days during which we first met. Telling each other, for the hundredth time about those days of bitter cold and endurance, in which friendships and love were forged in the white chill of ice…

A thought strikes me suddenly. 'That murder investigation. Remember?' I say. 'Well, there was something wrong about it.'

'What was that?' Sacha asks.

'They never thought to interview us. Not Braslav. Not myself.'

'Well,' Andrea says, 'Did you do it?'

'Do the murder? Of course not,' I say, and laugh. 'Neither of us would ever have done a thing like that. Neither of us ever would. We wouldn't harm a fly.'

'Well there you are, then,' Andrea says, and laughs.

But Braslav says sombrely, 'All men are capable of killing their fellows when it comes to it.'

Braslav…

Laughter has been dying across Europe since that night. Today is the first day of September. News has come on the radio that Adolph Hitler's troops have entered Poland in an act of aggression. The French and British governments are considering their response.

Nedim and I have lived through one war already. We were young teenagers: I was seventeen, Nedim just fourteen when the Archduke Ferdinand was shot. The fossilised government of Emperor Franz Josef made some effort to recruit a whole generation of young men for the cause that had just been stirred up. In contrast to the successful recruitment campaigns of Germany, England and France, the Empire's was a damp squib. I have to say, thank God – and thank you, Franz Josef – for that. I didn't fight. I stayed on my mother's farm and tended her cattle instead. The same went for Nedim. We talked about this, of course. We had lived separate lives back then. But now we do not.

I have to slip my heart onto my sleeve at this point and simply say it. Meeting Nedim changed my life. The first twelve hours I spent with him taught me all I have ever needed to know about love. In the days that followed – and in the years that have followed those – I learned about being needed by another person and needing that person in my turn.

Before I met Nedim I must have been a very small person. Sometimes, I think, no bigger or braver than a mouse that takes fright when the wind crackles a dry leaf. But once I had Nedim at my side I became the bravest of men. For him I would have faced down a whole pack of wolves and fought them with my bare teeth if someone hadn't pulled a timely trigger first.

Love. It's about giving: that's what love is. It's as simple as that. Curiously, that is exactly what I was taught as a child at school and in church by the priests. They may have been way off-beam when it came to understanding the intricacies of less usual kinds of human relationships but about love they were absolutely right.

Loving. Giving. That's what Nedim and I have done – have tried to do – for the past decade. And side by side we are ready to take on the world. We can not guess what the coming year is going to hold for us. We know only one thing for certain and it is this.

That not war, not life, not death itself shall tear us apart.

VALETE

Eduard...

Forgive me. My intrusion into this story must come as a rude shock. Not only have I headed my contribution to the story of Nedim and Braslav with my own name – a name that has not so far featured in their story once – but I have given this final, tacked-on, chapter a Latin title. The English translation of *valete*, like *vale,* is farewell or goodbye, of course. But *valete* carries an extra meaning with it. It is a farewell addressed to more than one person. This short addition to their story, then, is my loving farewell – and your farewell too, dear reader – to Nedim and Braslav.

I will introduce myself briefly, acutely conscious that it is not my story that you want to read about. I am the only son of Andrea, who features prominently in the story of Nedim and Braslav, and was a lifelong friend of the pair. Andrea, my father, inherited their property when they died, just a few weeks apart, in 1987 – when they were themselves both in their eighties. Braslav had once written touchingly: *What would it be like when two people as much in love as Nedim and I were died at the same time? Would it be like walking through a doorway together, hand in hand? Finding ourselves still holding hands in a sun-warmed flower-filled garden on the other side of it? For there was no possibility that a different, separate Paradise awaited people of Nedim's faith and people of mine. As Sacha had said, all routes to truth led to the same place, just as all railway lines converged on Trieste.*

They walked through that doorway just a shadow's breadth apart.

Their estate included the house they bought in Trieste when they retired from the Compagnie in the mid nineteen-sixties. It also included a mound of writings, including journals and diaries. It has taken me much time to sift this wealth of autobiography. I have done my best to find the important threads of their early story, and to shape it into the account you have just read. Much of the material was written in Serbo-Croat and some in German and, later, French. I have taken pains to translate it – with a little help from international friends – into English. Unsatisfactorily, inevitably. They wrote in the idiom of that time when they were young, the end of the 1920s and the start of the '30s, and I have tried to preserve their idiom in my translation, though sometimes with mixed results! Also, I have felt that their personalities sang clearly through their words in their original languages, and that some of this has inevitably become lost.

Braslav and Nedim remained a couple until the end of their long lives. That is probably the most important thing I have to write. Unless it is this: that throughout that time they remained deeply in love. I knew them well, first as a child and then as an adult, and I know that was the case.

Compared to that overwhelmingly important fact the details of the rest of their lives together seem minor. Nevertheless I shall briefly set them out.

They continued to work for the Compagnie as driver and fireman and part-time archivists until the outbreak of War in 1939 and the invasion of France in 1940 put a stop to the Orient Express services one by one. They attempted to enlist in the French army but due to some bureaucratic doubts occasioned by their Balkan nationalities, were not accepted. They went to work then, for the duration of the Second World War, for what was left of the French Railways, at a major locomotive and carriage depot in Eastern France: in a small town called Chalindrey, near Langres and not far from the Swiss border.

During this time they worked also for the French Resistance. They told me that, and I have no reason to doubt them. But they gave me few details and no written accounts of their exploits in this area of their life together have come to light among their papers. No doubt, if they had done, I should now find myself editing a second book. They did however tell me this. That some of the work they were engaged in involved the blowing up of trains. People were killed. They had that on their consciences, they told me. They killed, they said, as soldiers the world over have said since the dawn of history, that others might live. They told me they were not very comfortable with that. I can't say that I was.

Easier to deal with was the fact that they often found themselves destroying Wagons-Lits carriages that they had hauled in years gone by: carriages that had now been taken over and used by the German rail company Mitropa. They shrugged their shoulders in a shared gesture of resignation when they told me that. Shared gestures was one of the things they were good at.

Following the cessation of hostilities in 1945 the Orient Express gradually resumed its services across Europe. Braslav and Nedim were invited to re-join the Compagnie; they accepted the invitation gladly and returned to Paris. No longer riding the rails they continued to work on the Compagnie archive, and between them they occupied a variety of administrative posts. In 1960 – coincidentally the year of my birth – they were given seats on the board and became directors of the company for which they had now worked for forty years. They discovered the world of foreign business trips and holidays, incidentally fulfilling Nedim's assurance to Braslav – completely unfounded at the time he made it – that they would see both England and America before they died.

They retired from the Compagnie in 1965 and bought a house near the sea in Trieste – it was something they had always hankered after – not far from the place of my father's birth. During the first years of their retirement, when steam trains still worked the Yugoslavian railway routes, they were delighted from time to time to see a familiar locomotive hauling the northbound Orient Express into Trieste station. Its number was 72619, as you will already have guessed.

I knew that they were half-brothers. They told me that

and I didn't have a problem with it. I knew that they told some people that they were brothers when that suited them. To a different set of people, to those who were closer to them in temperament, they would admit to being lovers. To these they would explain that the brothers story was a smokescreen: the ink that the octopus colours the water with when it needs to protect itself in a hostile environment. To only a very select handful of people did they admit to being both. I count myself honoured to have been among that small group.

Life is wonderfully more complicated and surprising than we can ever expect, do you not think?

My father Andrea was gay, as you will know from Braslav's and Nedim's accounts. His long-time partner Sacha died in 1958, at the age of sixty-seven, three years after the start of his retirement. Andrea, still a sprightly fifty-year-old, and lonely in Paris without Sacha, met and – perhaps surprisingly – married a French woman, Isabelle, a year afterwards. A year after that she became my mother. As I have not quite just written, life is more wonderful – I mean more full of wonders – than we can comprehend or contemplate.

I am gay, by the way, in case you are wondering that. It's nothing special: not something I am proud of any more than it's something I am ashamed about. Braslav and Nedim were … I suppose the fashionable word is 'role-models' … to me. Knowing them from childhood onwards made it easier for me to grow up understanding who I was and accepting it. 'It's like the weather,' Nedim – my Uncle Ned – said to me once. 'The sun shines, the rain comes, the snow comes, and whatever comes we are stuck with it. In the case of the snow, sometimes actually stuck *in* it.' He laughed at his weak joke: it was a habit of his.

As you already know, Nedim was fond of quoting Shakespeare. I shall end with the quote he came out with on that occasion. It is from King Lear, I think.

He that hath and a little tiny wit,

With hey, ho, the wind and the rain,

Must make content with his fortunes fit,

For the rain, it raineth every day.

April 2015. Trieste

THE END

****

Anthony McDonald is the author of over twenty novels. He studied modern history at Durham University, then worked briefly as a musical instrument maker and as a farmhand before moving into the theatre, where he has worked in every capacity except director and electrician. He has also spent several years teaching English in Paris and London. He now lives in rural East Sussex.

Novels by Anthony McDonald

SILVER CITY

THE DOG IN THE CHAPEL

TOM & CHRISTOPHER AND THEIR KIND

RALPH: DIARY OF A GAY TEEN

IVOR'S GHOSTS

ADAM

BLUE SKY ADAM

GETTING ORLANDO

ORANGE BITTER, ORANGE SWEET

ALONG THE STARS

WOODCOCK FLIGHT

MATCHES IN THE DARK: 13 Tales of Gay Men

(Short story collection)

Gay Romance Series:

Sweet Nineteen

Gay Romance on Garda

Gay Romance in Majorca

The Paris Novel

Gay Romance at Oxford

Gay Romance at Cambridge

The Van Gogh Window

Gay Tartan

Tibidabo

Spring Sonata

Touching Fifty

Romance on the Orient Express

All titles are available as Kindle ebooks and as paperbacks from Amazon.

www.anthonymcdonald.co.uk